Moon Pie

www.**davidficklingbooks**.co.uk

Also by Simon Mason:

The Quigleys
The Quigleys at Large
The Quigleys Not for Sale
The Quigleys in a Spin

Simon Mason

David Fickling Books

OXFORD · NEW YORK

31 Beaumont Street
Oxford OX1 2NP, UK

MOON PIE
A DAVID FICKLING BOOK 978 0 385 61851 9

Published in Great Britain by David Fickling Books,
A Random House Group Company

This edition published 2011

1 3 5 7 9 10 8 6 4 2

The Random House Group Limited supports the Forest Stewardship Council (FSC),
the leading international forest certification organization. All our titles that are
printed on Greenpeace-approved FSC-certified paper carry the FSC logo. Our paper
procurement policy can be found at www.rbooks.co.uk/environment.

Mixed Sources
Product group from well-managed
forests and other controlled sources
www.fsc.org   Cert no. TT-COC-2139
© 1996 Forest Stewardship Council

Set in 12/16pt Goudy Old Style by
Falcon Oast Graphic Art Ltd.

DAVID FICKLING BOOKS
31 Beaumont Street, Oxford, OX1 2NP

www.kidsatrandomhouse.co.uk
www.rbooks.co.uk

Addresses for companies within The Random House Group Limited can be found
at: www.randomhouse.co.uk/offices.htm

THE RANDOM HOUSE GROUP Limited Reg. No. 954009

A CIP catalogue record for this book is available from the British Library.

Printed and bound in Great Britain by Clays Ltd, St Ives plc

*This book is in memory of Gary Conway (1961–2009)
and Philip Atkins (1950–2009).*

1

'Come down at once!' Martha called. 'You'll fall and hurt yourself.'

Dad took no notice. He went further up the drainpipe, grunting noisily, and grabbed the guttering of the bay window roof. With a sudden, wild effort he hoicked a leg over, and hung there like a gibbon, grinning fiercely down at them over his shoulder.

He panted something.

'What did he say, Martha?' Tug said.

'Pardon?' Martha called up.

'Piece of,' Dad said. 'Cake.'

He spoke like that, in short gasps. 'Done this. Before. No need. To worry.'

He took his hand off the guttering and began to wave, and quickly put it back again.

'Dad's strange, isn't he, Martha?' Tug said.

'He's very badly behaved. Dad, I want you to come down now. I'm going to go and get the spare key from Mrs Wilkinson.'

But Dad was already crouching on the steeply sloping bay window roof.

'Be careful!' Martha called.

He rose slowly to his feet, skittered suddenly on the tiles, waved his arms wildly once, and clung to the brickwork in front of him, laughing.

'Easy does it,' he said.

He shuffled sideways, face squashed against the brick, and blindly reached up an arm until he could feel the window sill of Martha's bedroom above him.

'Watch this, Tug,' he said over his shoulder. 'Any second now you're going to see me give a little jump. And grab hold of that sill. Pull myself up. Jimmy the sash. Ease open the window. And hey presto.'

Tug let go of Martha's hand. 'Do it, Dad!' he shouted. He began to dance with excitement.

Martha took back Tug's hand. 'Dad! You're to come down now. This minute!' She used her strictest voice.

'First, a little jump,' Dad said. He gave a little jump and missed the sill.

'Oh!' he said, as he fell.

He fell, crumpling onto the bay window roof, slithered crossways, scrabbling at the tiles, and skidded over the edge. He fell with a crunch into the hawthorn, which he had been promising to prune for months, and fell out of the hawthorn onto the wheelie bin which at once tipped over and flung him sideways along the gravel to where Martha and Tug stood holding hands and shouting.

Dad groaned, and there was a sudden silence, as if all the noise had been sucked out of the air. He lay there quietly on his back, eyes shut, bleeding from the nose. 'Well,' he said without opening his eyes. 'I think my cat-burglar days are over.'

Tug fell on him with a sob.

Lights came on in the windows of neighbours' houses and Martha took charge.

'Yes, a slight accident,' she was saying. 'No thank you, Mrs Wilkinson, I think he's OK. But may we use our spare key for a minute?'

Dad sat in the kitchen in his boxer shorts, with his left hand in a bowl of warm water and a large sticking plaster on his forehead. Martha was putting an ice pack round his right knee. The kitchen was small and square, with terracotta floor tiles, cracked here and there, and pine cupboards, a little shabby, and a much-repaired wooden table. There wasn't quite enough room for things, but it didn't matter because they could always be left on the counter or piled up in the corners or pushed behind the door.

'You'll need to see the doctor in the morning,' Martha said.

'I'm OK. Surface wounds. Nothing compared to the damage done to my pride. What do you think, Tug? Am I OK?'

'You bashed the tree,' Tug said. 'You broke the bin. The bin won't work now. Why did you break the bin?'

'I've been meaning to break that bin for weeks. I don't like that bin.'

'Why don't you like that bin?'

'It's rude and unhelpful. Ow!'

'Hold still,' Martha said. 'Don't listen to him, Tug. He knows he's been silly.'

'She's right, Tug. I've been very silly. And now look at me.'

They looked at him, where he sat, looking back at them glassily. There were cuts down his cheek where the hawthorn had scratched him and grazes on the backs of his hands and knees. Dust and dirt in his hair made him look suddenly older. But he was still Dad. Limping to the sink, he poured himself a glass of water, gingerly sipped it and pulled a funny face.

'What time is it?' he said.

'Midnight.'

'Come on then, or you'll be tired tomorrow. I'm going up now. Tug?'

'Yes, Dad?'

'You weren't frightened, were you? When I fell.'

'No.'

'Good boy.'

'I didn't like the noise.'

'No. I must remember to be silent when I fall off roofs.'

'But I wasn't frightened.'

'Good.'

Tug began to sniff.

'Come on, Tug,' Martha said. 'Upstairs.'

They all went up together, into the darkness of the unlit landing, and Dad said goodnight and limped into his room. In the bathroom Martha made sure Tug cleaned his teeth. He was so floppy with sleepiness she had to hold him upright at the wash basin on his plastic step. Then she helped him to his room, the smallest bedroom, tucked away at the end of the landing, and read him one page of a story, and settled him down.

'Good night, Tug.'

'Good night, Martha. Is the light on?'

She switched on the nightlight. 'Yes, the light's on.'

'Martha?'

'Yes, Tug?'

'Why's Dad strange?'

Before she answered she drew her eyebrows together into a little frown, which was something she did when she was puzzled or upset. Then she said, 'He's not really strange, Tug. He's just a bit excitable tonight. Go to sleep now.'

Going along the hall to her own room, she got into bed and lay there in the dark. A little while later she heard Dad get up and limp slowly back downstairs to the kitchen. She turned over and tried to get to sleep.

2

It was a warm summer's night, and it was hard to sleep. Throwing off the duvet, Martha got out of bed and went to stand at the window. She was a slender girl, not very tall for her age, with long straight hair the colour of copper, grey eyes and a small pointed nose that she seemed to be pointing at people when she looked at them. Standing there in her pyjamas, her chin level with the window sill, she lifted her head and pointed her nose at the moon, and its light fell over her in a silvery veil and made her pale face paler.

The roundish moon was bruised with shadow. *Like an old piece of china*, she thought. *Like a cracked bowl.*

After a while she went to see if Tug was OK, but even before she reached his room she heard him growling softly in his sleep. He was lying on his back with his fists up by the side of his head like a baby, smiling to himself. She wiped his hot hair off his face. He was only five, and he liked sleeping.

But I'm eleven, Martha thought. *So that's OK.*

On the way back to her room, she listened at the top of the stairs to check if Dad was still in the kitchen, and heard him, and went back to bed and lay there again, looking at the old bowl of the moon, thinking.

Tug was right. Dad *was* behaving strangely – clowning around, making fun of everything, having accidents. And it was odd, because he hadn't always been like that. He used to be calmer and quieter. Safer.

She lay there remembering what Dad had been like before he was strange.

She remembered him teaching her to play tennis when she was small. He wrapped his arm round her, and his big, sensible hand held her little hand holding the racket and swung it for her, and when she turned she felt his face against hers, warm and raspy, smelling of the pear drops he was always sucking. She remembered how safe it made her feel. In the past Dad had always been quietly *there* – in the house or the garden where they could find him. Now he was nowhere in particular, and at the same time, unexpectedly, all over the place. He wasn't very quiet or sensible either. He sang songs at the top of his voice, and played boisterous games, and climbed up the front of the house when he locked himself out. Sometimes he got angry for no reason. Over the last few months he had become loud and risky and forgetful. Just that evening he had forgotten to talk to Tug's teacher after school, and had forgotten to make tea, and had forgotten to pick Martha up from Costumes Club, and when, in the end, she called to remind him, he had been in such a mad rush to leave the house he had forgotten his key.

Sometimes he seemed to be rushing everywhere, yet at other times he had no energy at all. Although he was full of great plans for things to do, he generally stayed in his dressing gown until lunch time. It was very odd.

Perhaps it's because he doesn't have a job any more, Martha thought. *And it makes him strange.*

She frowned. She was going to have to make sure things didn't get out of hand. After all, you can't have everyone acting strange. Someone has to keep their head, and if it wasn't going to be Dad, it would have to be her.

She looked out of the window, but the moon was gone. She was too sleepy to worry any more, and she finally closed her eyes. The last thing she heard before she fell asleep was Dad coming up the stairs whistling.

3

The doctors' surgery was across the park, by a little lake. There were coots on the lake, and swans and geese. The geese were noisy: sometimes they screamed like babies.

'I don't like gooses,' Tug said.

'Geese,' Martha said.

'Don't like gooses myself,' Dad said. 'Dirty birds. Perhaps,' he added, 'I shall tell the doctor that one of his gooses attacked me.'

He limped along the gravel path, wincing and occasionally stumbling. One of his eyes had closed up, and he wore dark glasses to hide the bruising.

As they walked along, Martha looked at him. It wasn't just the bruising that made him look odd. He didn't look well. His sandy hair, which used to be so thick and springy, was flat and shiny, and his face was pale and shadowy, and in general he looked sort of diluted.

Martha frowned. 'They're not his geese, Dad.'

'No, but he's their friend. I've seen him feeding them.'

It was a sunny Saturday morning. The park was full of people: members of the rowing club plying their skiffs on the water; old men in cardigans standing around the boating pond where they raced their model boats; joggers going round and round the paths. All the tennis courts were busy. There were people walking their dogs and pushing their bikes along and standing talking; some were even sunbathing on the lawns.

'Don't expect him to do anything for me, by the way,' Dad said. 'Doctors don't like to do much if they can help it.'

Dr Woodley was a grey-haired man with a large, pale face held together by a pair of thin steel spectacles, and he didn't like to do much, as he often told them.

'You're ill,' he would say. 'But you'll get better. It's dull being ill, Lord knows, but it won't last long. Come back if you start coughing up blood.'

They went into Dr Woodley's surgery, and Dad sat gingerly on a chair, and Martha sat on the bed, and Tug lay on the floor making noises and moving earth with his best JCB. It was real earth which he had

11

picked up in the park, but Dr Woodley didn't seem to mind.

He peered at Dad. 'Cats?' he asked. 'Or did your children beat you up?'

'Fell off a roof.'

'Looks painful.' He began to examine Dad's face. 'Minor abrasions. Some contusion. Nice black eye. Really, very nice. Won't last long though. Let's have a look at your leg.'

Dad took off his trousers and lay on the bed.

'Not as bad as I feared when I saw you limp in. Did you ice it?'

'I iced it,' Martha said.

Dr Woodley peered at her. 'Clever girl.'

'Someone has to keep their head,' she said, with a glance at Dad.

Dr Woodley looked thoughtful. He wrote out a prescription for antiseptic ointment, and then he said, 'We've seen quite a lot of you recently, Mr Luna.'

Dad shrugged.

'Let's have a look at the records. Psoriasis flaring up. That was in February. Blurred vision at the beginning of March. Migraine and gastric upset in April. What's this? Last month you had what you thought was a hernia.'

'Turned out to be indigestion,' Dad said.

'And now you've fallen off a roof. You've been in the wars. Hardly saw you at all for years, then suddenly every month.'

'Just a run of bad luck. I'm pretty fit in general.'

Dr Woodley peered at him silently. 'I think what I'll do,' he said at last, 'is take a quick sample for a blood test. Just to make sure you haven't picked up an infection from those cuts.'

'All right.'

A few moments later they were ready to leave. Dr Woodley shook hands with them all, even Tug, whose hand contained quite a lot of earth.

'Look after yourself,' he said to Dad. 'Or perhaps,' he said to Martha, 'I should ask *you* to look after him.'

They walked back across the park.

'What an old crock I am,' Dad said. 'I can't go on like this. Things will have to change. Tell you what, how would you like us to live on a boat? I think things would be better if we lived on the water. Fresher, cleaner, more exciting.'

Tug stopped making JCB noises. 'What sort of boat?'

'A canal boat. One of those long, thin ones we see

at the lock. It'd be like camping. When we get bored with one place, we just move somewhere else. We could move right out of the city. Imagine waking up among the fields. No traffic, just the birds and the cows and the early-morning mist. And walking into the nearest village for breakfast.'

'Let's do it!' Tug shouted.

'What about school?' Martha said.

'Take a year off,' Dad said. 'Nothing easier.'

'But how will you get a new job if we keep moving?'

'We'll be runaways. Fugitives. Always one step ahead. Popping up here, popping up there.'

'And what will we do about money?'

Dad sighed.

They came to the street and walked along swinging Tug between them until they reached their house.

'You know your problem?' Dad said to Martha. 'You're too serious.' He began to look through his pockets. 'Where's that key?'

'In my purse.' She gave it to him. 'I think I should look after the key from now on.' She gave Dad a firm look.

Dad patted her head. 'I expect you're right.' He yawned. 'You know, I'm still tired after our adventures last night. Will you wake me up for lunch?'

He limped upstairs.

Tug followed Martha into the kitchen. 'Martha?'

'Yes, Tug.'

'What shall we call it?'

'What shall we call what?'

'What shall we call our boat?'

'We're not going to get a boat.'

'But Dad said.'

'Dad didn't mean it.'

'Why didn't Dad mean it?'

Martha didn't reply. She didn't know the answer. In any case, she was already getting out the dustpan and brush. Over the last few months – ever since Dad started to be strange – she had taken charge of the housework.

'You have to help me now, Tug,' she said. 'First tidying, then cleaning, then lunch. What do you want for lunch?'

'Lots.'

'Lots of what?'

'Lots of lunch.' Tug was always hungry.

'OK. Think about it while you sweep.'

As usual, Martha made a timetable in her head:

Do housework.

Make lunch.

Sew.
Go to Marcus's.
Help Dad with tea.
Bath Tug.
Read to Tug.
Go to bed.

'Come on,' she said to Tug. 'We haven't got all day.'

Together they swept the kitchen floor, and emptied the bin, and cleaned the sink, and afterwards they tidied the front room. They drew back the curtains and opened windows, and sunlight came in and glittered in the dust of the air. The street outside was quiet, and as they worked they heard birdsong from the gardens around, high-pitched sparrows and broken-voiced pigeons. It was a small house, with a front room, a back room and a kitchen downstairs, two and a half bedrooms upstairs, and a strip of garden at the back divided equally into broken patio, rank undergrowth and collapsing shed. They had only lived there a few months, and it didn't feel like home yet. There was 'work to be done', mainly to the plumbing, which squeaked and roared, and to the kitchen, which was damp. Dad hadn't got round to doing the work yet.

'Pie,' Tug said at last.

'We haven't got pie. How about fish fingers?'

'All right. How many?'

'Four.'

'All right. Is there ketchup?'

'Lots of ketchup. Go and wake Dad, and I'll start cooking.'

Martha liked cooking. For Tug she cooked simple food like fish fingers, but she preferred to do more complicated things, like macaroni cheese or shepherd's pie or hotpot. She was very good at *Spaghetti alla Carbonara*, which was one of Dad's favourites. At Cookery Club she was learning to make quite sophisticated dishes. For her, cooking was a sort of game – a slow, patient game you played on your own. And the nicest thing about it was that while you played it you didn't have to think about anything else.

Sometimes – she thought – it was a relief not to have to think about things.

Tug came back down with the news that Dad would not be woken.

'I bashed his foot a bit,' he said. 'But he didn't stop sleeping.'

So Martha and Tug had lunch on their own, and Tug ate seven fish fingers with a quarter of a pint of ketchup. Afterwards he played in the garden, keeping away from the undergrowth where the broken glass was, while Martha sewed up the hole in Dad's trousers.

At three o'clock she put away the sewing box and said briskly, 'Now it's time to play with Marcus. You have to come with me, Tug.'

'Why?' Tug was suspicious of Marcus.

'Because Dad's still asleep, and I can't leave you here because you'll get into mischief.'

Tug looked interested. 'What mischief?'

Martha sighed. 'If you come to Marcus's with me I'll buy you a lolly at the shop on the way.'

'Do they sell pies?' ·

'No. Lollies. You like lollies.'

'All right.'

They left a note for Dad written by both of them. It said: *Hope you had a NIS SLEEEEEP. Gone to MarKISS KISS KISS. Back for tea. Love Martha AND TUG XXXX*. Then they set off down the street.

For a while they walked quietly, holding hands. Martha was carrying a large bag and Tug was carrying his JCB, which he talked to from time to time.

'Why didn't Dad wake up?' he asked again.

'He's very tired after falling off the roof last night.'

Tug yawned.

They walked down the street into the park and across the grass, avoiding the geese.

'He *is* strange, isn't he, Martha?'

She admitted it.

'But he's not as strange as Marcus. Is he, Martha?'

'No one is as strange as Marcus, Tug.'

4

Marcus's house was small and ordinary, which was odd because Marcus was neither.

He opened the door, and stood there looking down at them. He was a large, solid boy with dark hair, and he was dressed in a pair of tights and a lime-green beret. He seemed to be wearing make-up.

'Have you got them?' he asked Martha. He spoke in a breathless, theatrical voice.

She held up the bag, and he took it and smiled. Then he noticed Tug.

'Is your brother on his way somewhere?'

Martha explained.

For a moment Marcus looked disappointed. But he recovered. 'There are some parts for small, grubby children,' he said. 'I'd forgotten. We can use him. We can use you,' he added, loudly, to Tug. He always spoke to Tug as if he was deaf.

'Come up to the studio,' he said.

'He *is* stranger than Dad, isn't he?' Tug whispered to Martha. He sounded impressed.

'Much stranger,' Martha whispered back.

On the way they passed Marcus's mum and dad, and said hello. Marcus's mum worked at Tesco and his dad was a postman, and they were both quiet, nervous people. They seemed especially nervous of Marcus.

'You know Martha already,' he told them, waving a hand. 'The costume designer. Her brother, an urchin. By the way,' he went on, 'we'll be recording, so keep the noise down please. And can we have tea and biscuits at four?'

They left his parents nodding silently and smiling in a bewildered way at the bottom of the stairs, and went up after Marcus to the studio, which was his bedroom.

It did not look like a bedroom. The curtains were drawn very tightly to exclude all light and in a space cleared round the bed were a large white screen, several spotlights on tripods and a camcorder on an aluminium cradle. Everywhere else there were clothes and stage props and theatrical make-up.

'Martha?' Tug said quietly.

'Yes, Tug.'

'Why does he move his arms round like that?'

'He only does it when he talks. Don't stand too close.'

Martha sat on the edge of the bed. Tug found the camcorder.

Marcus said loudly, 'Back away from the equipment please.'

From the bed Tug watched Marcus try on the clothes that Martha had brought in front of a full-length mirror on the back of the door. He put on a pair of grey trousers, then a brown velvet-look jacket and then a cravat. He smiled at himself.

'This is very good, Martha,' he said over his shoulder. 'Very nice, very Henry Higgins. I only wish . . .'

'Wish what?' Martha said.

'I only wish you could have used something a bit more colourful. Just a bit more adventurous. This brown.'

'What about the brown?'

'It's a good brown. But it doesn't hit you. Doesn't knock your eye out.'

'You wanted it to look old,' Martha said, a little crossly.

'And I like it,' Marcus said. 'I like it very much. I particularly like the stitching,' he said soothingly.

'But I wonder if we could make it a teensy bit live-
lier. What about some fur round the collar? You can
get some good artificial fur in electric blue, I've
seen it.'

While Marcus and Martha talked, Tug sidled over
to the camcorder again. It was very shiny, with lots of
inviting buttons, and although it was quite big it
didn't look very heavy, and Tug was just testing how
heavy it really was when he felt himself being picked
up and put back on the bed.

'Now I know why you're called Tug,' Marcus said.
'I'm afraid I cannot allow the urchins to handle the
equipment,' he said to Martha.

'But I like equipment,' Tug said.

'I have another use for him,' Marcus said. 'I have
another use for you,' he said loudly to Tug, who was
watching his hands and managed to dodge them.
'Have you heard of a thing called *My Fair Lady*?'

Tug shook his head.

Marcus spoke loudly and slowly. '*My Fair Lady* is a
film. A movie from days long ago. A great classic.
Nod if you understand me.'

Tug nodded doubtfully.

'Your sister and I are remaking it. Here, in my
studio. A speed version. If you listen carefully I will

tell you the story. Then you will help us remake it. Do you have any questions?'

'When will the biscuits get here?' Tug said.

Marcus told the story of *My Fair Lady*. It involved a bad-tempered gentleman teaching a poor girl how to talk in a posh voice. There were songs, apparently funny, and some dancing.

'I will play the posh old gentleman,' Marcus said. 'His name is Henry Higgins, and he wears a jacket of brown velvet which may or may not be trimmed with blue fur. I will also play the poor girl, who is called Eliza Doolittle. She wears a variety of dresses.'

He looked at Martha.

'In the bag,' she said. 'I haven't made the petticoat yet.'

Marcus turned back to Tug. 'I am going to let you appear in the very first scene. You will play the part of a street urchin. You will be dirty and badly-behaved. There is no need to act. You will sing a song. The song is called "Wouldn't it be Loverly".'

'Wouldn't it be what?'

Stepping backwards into the area enclosed by the white screen, Marcus began to sing. As he sang, he pranced to and fro. The song was full of words like 'abso-bloomin'-lutely', which made no sense, and noises like the sound of someone having his nose tweaked, and the whole thing was terrible.

Marcus came to an end. 'Do you think you can sing that?'

Tug shook his head firmly.

'Well, what can you sing?'

Tug thought for a moment. '"The Bear Went Over the Mountain".'

'How does that go?'

Tug sang in a shy, gruff monotone: 'The bear went over the mountain, the bear went over the mountain, the bear went over the mountain.'

Marcus nodded. 'All right, that'll do. Shall we start?'

'Martha?' Tug said.

'Yes, Tug.'

'Why aren't you playing?'

'I don't much like playing, Tug.'

Then they started.

When tea and biscuits arrived, Marcus told them to 'take five', and Tug took five biscuits, and they sat on the bed listening to Marcus talk about becoming a celebrity.

'But I will remember you,' he said. 'I will write about you in my memoirs.'

His memoirs were already in their third volume. He wrote them mainly in Maths on Wednesday and Friday afternoons, and sometimes passed the pages to Martha – who sat next to him – for safe-keeping.

After a while he told Tug to move away from the camcorder again.

'But I like cameras,' Tug said. 'My dad used to work in a television studio, and they had lots of cameras there. And a canteen,' he said.

Marcus nodded. 'I know. I was hoping your dad might be able to help me get on in the movie indus- try. Has he got himself a new job yet?'

Martha shook her head.

'Why? Aren't there any?'

'He doesn't seem to want one at the moment.'

'Is he all right?'

For a moment Martha didn't know how to answer. 'Yes,' she said at last. She frowned.

'We're going to live on a boat,' Tug put in. 'In the fields.'

'Your brother's quite a fantasist, isn't he? Quite a little dreamer of dreams, aren't you?'

'I like to sleep,' Tug said.

'I was impressed with the way he handled himself

in scene one,' Marcus said to Martha. 'Despite the risk to the equipment.'

'I like equipment,' Tug said stubbornly.

'I know you do, little Tug. But does it like you?'

'You're strange,' Tug said.

'Of course I am. Do you think you can be a celebrity without making a spectacle of yourself? Now I must change for the next scene. Martha, tell me honestly: do you think the tea gown will work without the petticoat?'

5

Martha and Tug walked past their schools, first Martha's, then Tug's, both empty now at the weekend. Martha's school was large and grey, and she liked it. She was in Year Seven. She wore a blue uniform, and was good at Maths and famous for red hair and neatness. Marcus was her best friend, but she got on well with everyone. Tug's school was small and grey, and he was bored of it. He was in Year One and looking forward to finishing schooling as soon as possible. He was famous for eating and a trick he did with spit.

Beyond their schools was the park again. It was still busy. Some families were having picnics on the grass between the flowerbeds.

They went by the doctors' surgery and along the outer path until they came to the library. Every Saturday they came here to exchange their books.

'What are you going to get out, Tug?'

He took a book out of the book-bin.

'The Very Hungry Caterpillar? Again?'

'It makes me feel happy.'

'All right. Choose some others too. I'm going to choose mine over here.'

After half an hour they left the library and went back into the park on their way home.

'Will we have a picnic today?' Tug asked.

'I don't know. Dad's making tea.'

'I like picnics.'

'I know you do.'

'I like sausages for my picnics. And pies. And crisps. And scotch eggs. And sausage rolls. And chicken.' He thought hard for a while. 'Oh, and pies,' he added.

'We'll have to see what Dad has got ready for us.'

'What do you like for your picnics, Martha?'

'I don't really mind.'

'Do you like pies?'

'Yes, I suppose so.'

'What sort of pies?'

'I don't know, Tug. Let's talk about something else.'

'Like what?'

'I don't know.'

They walked round the edge of the lake, avoiding the geese.

'Do you like our new house, Tug?' she said at last.

'No.'

'Why not?'

He stared at her in surprise. 'It's small, Martha, and it's always broken. I liked our old house,' he added in a low voice.

Martha was cross. 'You're not to say that. I've told you before. It doesn't do any good.'

'All right. But I did,' he added. Tug could be very stubborn. 'I liked my old room,' he said quietly.

Martha ignored him.

'I liked the play den,' he said. 'I liked the tennis court.'

'Shh, Tug.'

They walked on in silence. But Martha couldn't help thinking about their old house too. It was a big stone house up on a hill above the city, with its own orchard and an acre of woodland, and they had been very happy there. Dad hadn't been strange then. In fact – now she thought about it – Dad wasn't a bit strange until they moved into their new house – as if he had somehow left himself behind at the old house with the old carpets and curtains, and become someone else. But that didn't make sense.

She frowned.

They reached the park gates and went out into the streets.

'I liked the TV room,' Tug was whispering to himself. 'I liked the orchard.'

When they got home, they found the front door wide open and Dad gone. There was a note on the kitchen table. It said: *Had to go out. Sorry! Back soon – with a surprise! Love Dad.*

'What surprise, Martha? Will it be pies?'

'We'll have to see.' She looked at her watch, and thought about her timetable. 'I think we'd better have bath time while we wait.'

Tug gave her a dangerous look. 'But we haven't had tea. We never have baths before tea.' He was tired and cross and hungry. He looked as if he might be getting into one of his moods.

Martha felt the beginning of a headache coming on. 'Tonight it's bath first, then tea. When Dad gets back with his surprise.'

'I don't like it when there's no Dad,' Tug said.

'Don't worry. I'm here to look after you.'

'I don't like it when there's no *tea.*'

'There will be tea, Tug. You don't understand.'

'No, Martha. *You* don't understand. I'm hungry.'

'I know you are. You just have to wait a little while.'

Tug sat down on the floor. It was a bad sign.

'Tug!'

He sat cross-legged with his arms folded, his head bent and his shoulders hunched, scowling violently. He began to grumble to himself. This was another bad sign. Martha's headache got worse, and she put her hand on her forehead and counted to ten.

'Please, Tug.'

He scowled and grumbled and didn't move.

Martha lost her temper. 'You look like a block of old wood,' she said angrily. 'You're almost square. I've never noticed before how square you are. You ought to be careful someone doesn't come along and put you in a skip.'

He didn't stop scowling, but he began to sniff, and Martha felt sorry for him, he was so small and square, and his hair was so hot and messy. So she sat down next to him, and crossed her own legs and hunched her own shoulders and scowled to herself, and found that it felt quite nice. Then she sighed. 'What's your favourite sort of pie, Tug?'

After a while of not answering, he sniffed and muttered, 'Steak and kidney.'

Martha made a shocked noise. 'But I thought it was mince and onion.'

He turned to her at once. 'No, Martha, that's wrong. I like mince and onion. But I like steak and kidney better.'

'OK. I'm sorry, I made a mistake. If Dad's surprise isn't a steak and kidney pie, I'll make you one next week. How about that?'

Tug considered this. 'All right.'

'But you have to have a bath now. Is it a deal?'

'All right.'

'Come on then.'

They got up together and went upstairs, and Martha ran the bath while Tug sat on the toilet singing 'The Bear Went Over the Mountain' to himself.

'Marcus is strange, isn't he?' he said, and yawned.

After Tug's bath, Dad still wasn't back. Martha opened a can of beans and they had baked beans on toast together at the kitchen table. Then they played games, and finally they watched television. Night fell and it got dark. They put the lights on and drew the curtains, and Martha locked the back door.

'Why's Dad late, Martha?' Tug asked.

'I don't know. The surprise must take a long time to get ready.'

In the end she put Tug to bed herself. She read *The Very Hungry Caterpillar* with him, and tucked him in and put the nightlight on, and went along the landing to her own room.

For a while she stood at the window, peering out and listening. It was odd without Dad in the house. He left a silence in it. The silence was thin and fragile, like a silence about to be broken, and Martha listened to it, holding her breath and waiting for a noise, like the sound of Dad coming back. But there was no noise.

I'm eleven, she thought. *I shouldn't be frightened of the silence, or the dark. I have to keep my head, and not be silly.*

Settling herself on the carpet in a corner of her room, she read *Little Women*, which was one of the books she had borrowed from the library, occasionally lifting her head to listen out for Dad. Eventually she grew sleepy, and got into bed and lay there with her eyes closed. But the silence kept her awake. In the end she got up again and stood at the window in her dressing gown, looking at the moon.

Like a white pebble, she thought. *Like a bit of bone.*

She wished she could make it look more interesting, but she tried, and she couldn't.

Her bedside clock with the luminous face said 10.05 p.m., and she wondered where Dad was, and what he was doing. Several times recently he had come home late. One evening she had asked him where he had been, but he hadn't answered. He made a joke, as he often did when she asked him a question, and looked the other way and was silent.

Dad was like the moon. Hard to think about.

Suddenly the thought came to her that he might have been in the garden all this time, or in the shed at the bottom of the garden where he sometimes liked to potter, and although it was a silly idea she thought she should go and see.

The stairwell was dark, and the light wasn't working. At the top she hesitated, peering down, pointing her small nose all the way to the bottom. She couldn't see anything. Taking a deep breath, she tiptoed quietly down, listening out for anything that sounded like Dad, and at the bottom of the stairs she was startled by the telephone suddenly ringing, very loudly, down the hallway. She pulled herself off the wall, and ran towards it. *That must be him now*, she thought, and without knowing why she felt afraid of what he was going to say to her.

'Hello?'

'Hello? Who's that? Is it you, Martha?'

'Yes.'

'It's Grandma, Martha. What are you doing up so late? You sound as if you've been running. Are you watching a film?'

'No.'

'What are you doing?'

'Nothing. I was . . . I was just sitting here thinking.'

After she said this, Grandma was silent for a moment.

'May I talk to your father?'

Martha said, 'He's not here.'

There was another pause.

'Do you have a babysitter with you, Martha?'

'No.'

Grandma made a noise, and Martha said quickly. 'He'll be back any minute. He's just popped out. To see a friend down the road.'

This time she heard muffled noises, as if Grandma was holding her hand over the phone and talking to someone else.

'Will you ask him to telephone me as soon as possible?'

'Yes.'

'Tell him it's important. I'm anxious that he doesn't forget lunch next Sunday.'

'All right.'

When she put down the phone the house was quiet again, and she could almost hear her heart beating high up in her chest. Grandma was scary in a well-spoken sort of way, and Martha didn't like talking to her on the phone. Tug didn't like talking to her at all, and sometimes hid when she came round. She lived with Grandpa in a big house quite near.

But the phone call had broken the spell of the empty house. On her way to bed, Martha checked on Tug again, and found him in a purring heap under his duvet, flushed and damp-haired and deeply asleep. Then she went to bed herself, and to her surprise fell asleep almost straight away.

6

She woke in the dark with a gulp, and Dad said, 'Surprise!'

He was standing at the edge of the bed, shining a torch on himself and laughing, and she sat up with a cry. In the torchlight he didn't look like Dad at all, his face was criss-crossed with white stripes and black shadow, like warpaint.

'Dad?' she cried again.

Dad just laughed. 'And his torch,' he said.

'Why?'

'Because it's dark, of course. Can't see when it's dark. Everyone knows that.'

'Where have you been?' she asked.

'Up you get,' he said. 'Quickly.'

'Where are we going?'

'Out. Into the night. Into the beautiful summer night.'

Before she had time to think, she was getting dressed in the dark while Dad fetched Tug. Then they went downstairs together, Dad carrying Tug – still sleeping, wrapped in a blanket – and out of the house.

The street was bathed in faint orange light from the street lamps, and the sky above was pale dark, and everything was quiet. It was still warm, and the soft air smelled of singed dust. As they went down the street, Dad and Martha whispered to each other.

'What time is it, Dad?'

'Half past two.'

'Where did you go for so long?'

'You'll see.'

'Where are we going now?'

'You'll find out. Did you miss me?'

'Yes.'

'I missed you too. Isn't it a beautiful night? Shall we dance?'

He began to waltz down the street with Tug in his arms.

Martha remembered the phone call earlier, and called after him, 'You have to phone Grandma.'

He ignored her. 'Just wait till you see what I've got to show you.' His eyes were bright, and he sounded excited. He smiled to himself a lot. Once or twice he stumbled. 'Tug's got heavy,' he said, apologetically.

They went quietly to the end of the street, and

across the main road, and along the cycle track until they came to the park, an area of darkness beyond the street lamps.

'What are we doing here, Dad? It's all locked up.'

'I know a way in,' he said, and they went round the fence until they came to a kissing gate, where there was a gap in the railings.

'Kiss me,' he said, laughing.

Inside the park it was darker, and Martha hesitated. Sudden splashings from the lake echoed in the empty quietness.

Dad switched on his torch. 'This way. Follow me. Careful now. Watch out for an ambush.' He laughed.

Martha stayed where she was. Her heart was beating fast. 'Dad?'

He swung round and his torch made loops of light. All round them were things invisible in the darkness, and things moving invisibly.

'Come on, Martha!'

'What are we doing here? It's the middle of the night.'

He just laughed again. 'Don't you trust me?'

'I don't like the dark,' she whispered.

But he moved away, and she had to run to catch him up.

Holding on to the back of his shirt, she followed him along the path in darkness behind the beam of torchlight, from the path to the rough ground, and across the rough ground to the trees at the edge of the lake, and through the trees until they came to a grassy space, and stopped.

Dad shone his torch down, and she saw things laid out in tupperware boxes on a blue-and-white rug. Dad grinned.

'What's this?' Martha said.

'It's a picnic.'

'Whose picnic?'

'Ours, of course.'

She was astonished. 'When did you do it?'

'Earlier.'

'But, Dad. It's the middle of the night.'

'It's a midnight picnic.'

Dad settled Tug on a big cushion, still wrapped in his blanket, and began to open the boxes.

'Sausage rolls,' he said. 'Ham sandwiches. Crisps. Cheese straws. Scotch eggs. Little tomatoes. More crisps. What's this? Salad, very important. French bread. There's butter too, somewhere. Damn, I forgot a knife. Doughnuts. Cherries. Orange squash. And apple juice. There. Have I missed anything?'

'What's in the tin foil?'

'Ah, yes.'

Dad unwrapped the foil, and leaned over Tug and shook him gently until he woke. 'Look what we've got, Tug.'

Tug opened his eyes and stared all round in astonishment at the trees and sky, and at last looked at what Dad was holding. 'Whose pie is it?' he whispered.

'Your pie. Steak and kidney.'

Tug smiled and closed his eyes again. 'You came,' he whispered. 'You came with pie.' And he went straight back to sleep with his fingers resting on the warm pastry.

Dad had also brought some candles, and now he lit them and put them in the grass, and then Martha and Dad settled down on either side of Tug and began to eat.

'Have you ever had a midnight picnic before, Martha?'

'No.'

'Listen. How peaceful it is. So quiet.'

Tug woke up again with a grunt, and said, 'Where are we?' in a very surprised voice, as if he hadn't woken up before.

'In the land of pies,' Dad said. 'Which is in the park, near the lake. We're having a midnight picnic.'

'Where are the gooses?'

'Sleeping. If you listen, you'll probably hear one snore in a minute.'

Almost straight away there was a sudden splash from the other side of the lake, and a distant goose made a noise. It wasn't a scream. It was a friendly honk.

Tug began to eat. 'This is steak and kidney pie,' he said after a moment. 'And I was dreaming about steak and kidney pie. So Marcus was right.'

'Marcus?' Dad said. 'Marcus is a very strange boy.'

For a while they were all quiet, eating peacefully. Dad had calmed down. Martha was no longer scared. Her eyes were used to the darkness, and she saw that the night was made up of many different shades and shadows. They hung in the trees and stretched along the ground. The trees were flat and still, but the water of the lake streamed white-and-black with moonlight, and the air around her was soft and peppery and warm.

She looked across at Dad eating a sausage roll. Although he was behaving strangely, he was still Dad.

'Why are we having this picnic?'

'I thought you'd like it.'

'But why a midnight picnic?'

He thought about that for a while.

'Because you've never had one before. Which makes it special. And I thought you'd like to look at the stars, which is hard to do in the middle of the day. Look how many there are.' He looked up, sighing. 'I love coming here at night. Before you were born I used to come here a lot. It's a very special spot. Look, Tug. All the stars.'

'Why?' Tug said sleepily.

'Just because.'

'Just because why?'

'Just because I love you.'

Tug thought about that, while Dad laughed to himself.

'How much do you love me?' Tug said at last. It was a game they used to play.

'I love you more than . . . ham loves sandwiches.'

Tug said rapidly, 'I love you more than gooses love honks.'

Dad turned to Martha. 'And you, whatsyername, I love you more than butter loves bread.'

'And I love you more than fishes love water.'

'But I love you more than Tugs love pies.'

44

'That's a lot,' Martha said. 'I can't beat that.'

Finally she relaxed, and lay back on the grass and looked up at the night sky, and smiled to herself. *When I'm older*, she thought, *I'll remember this midnight picnic as a good thing. I'll forget that I was scared of the dark, and that Dad was strange. I'll remember the candles in the grass, like flowers made out of flame, and Tug dreaming of pie, and Dad telling me he loves me.*

She was glad to have sorted this out. She liked sorting things out in her mind.

She rolled onto her side and looked at Dad.

He's not all bad, she thought. *Perhaps I shouldn't tell him off so much.*

'There are lots of stories about the stars,' Dad said. 'But I don't know any.'

'Is there a story about the moon?' she asked thoughtfully.

'Not that I know of.'

'It looks like pie,' Tug said suddenly. 'Doesn't it, Martha?'

And when they had finished laughing they found that Tug had gone to sleep again.

Dad put his jacket round Martha, and they snuggled together.

'How mad am I?' he said. 'On a scale of one to ten?'

'Eleven.'

'A hundred and eleven,' he said. He sighed, and smiled. 'But I only do it because I love you.' He put his arm round her. 'I love you more than ... I love you more than dads usually love Marthas.'

'I know,' she said. 'I love you too.'

They sat together under his jacket. Ten minutes passed in silence, and Dad began to fidget.

'I like midnight picnics,' Martha said after a while. 'But, Dad? Why did you bring us *here*? Why is this a special spot?'

He didn't answer at once. He fidgeted. 'Well it's good for stars,' he said at last.

His voice was raspy suddenly, and he took his arm away from her and shifted his position.

'But why just here? You said you used to come here before we were born.'

He made a joke, and she asked him again. He said nothing. And then he looked the other way.

At that moment Martha guessed.

'You used to come here with Mum, didn't you?' she said. 'That's why.'

Dad didn't say anything. He just kept looking the other way.

7

When Martha was little her mum was an actress. She acted on the stage and on television, and for several years played a small role in one of the famous TV soaps, which is where she met Dad, who was Director of Photography for the show.

She was a pretty woman with red hair the same shade as Martha's, and very pale skin; people used to recognize her in the street. It was exciting Mum being on television. Sometimes Martha went with Dad to the studios to watch them filming Mum's show; and once Mum took her to an awards ceremony at the Dorchester Hotel, where she met lots of television people wearing extraordinary costumes who drank champagne all evening and told each other hilarious stories. Mum liked parties. She was always laughing.

At home, however, she could be surprisingly strict, much stricter than Dad. She was the one who made the family rules, and organized everyone, and kept everything under control. *Someone has to keep their head*, she used to say. She taught Martha to keep her room tidy, and be polite and pleasant to others, and go to bed promptly at bedtime. Once a week Martha helped cook tea. After Tug was born, Mum taught Martha how to feed and wash him and even change him, so that before long she was used to taking care of him.

But what Martha remembered best about Mum was her energy. Her liveliness. She had a way of walking, very purposeful, and a way of speaking, her words bright and clear, and a way of looking at people, frank and shiny-eyed. She always knew what to do, and what to say. She was a kind person, with firm views and a sense of fun, who liked dancing and was never ill.

Then, one day in late July two years ago, Mum drove down to Cornwall with Martha and Tug and Grandma for a week's holiday by the sea. Dad had to stay behind, to work. It was a long journey, hot and uncomfortable, and before they reached Bristol, Mum complained of feeling dizzy and sick. At Exeter, Grandma took over the driving, and Mum lay back in the passenger seat, trembling and breathing very fast. At Plymouth, Grandma was so worried she drove straight to the hospital, where Mum was taken immediately into Intensive Care, and Martha sat with Tug and a nurse in a waiting room. Eventually she fell asleep, but woke again, straight away it seemed, to find Grandma weeping on the seat next to her.

Tug was only three: he was more bewildered than upset. But Martha was nine, and she understood. She had a sudden dizzy feeling, like falling; as if she was falling down a hole, plummeting through darkness with nothing to hold on to and no air to breathe, falling and falling until she was so suffocated and squeezed that in the end she was sick on the floor. Afterwards, and even now, she got the dizzy feeling from time to time. It came on her unexpectedly, like a headache. Out of nowhere a thought of Mum would come into her head, and she would start to fall, and fall and fall, thinking of Mum until she was sick. When it happened, she told people she had a stomach bug. She didn't want to tell them what it really was.

Dad never talked about Mum. Straight after the funeral he cleared out her clothes and gave them away, and put all the photographs of her into the attic; he didn't even keep a picture for his room. Whenever Martha started to talk about Mum, he always changed the subject. He said they needed to move on. He had all the love that Martha and Tug needed, he said. But Martha knew he couldn't talk about Mum because he was so upset.

For about a year their routines stayed the same. Dad took Martha to school and Tug to playgroup, and went off to work at the television studio in the mornings. In the afternoons Grandma and Grandpa picked them up from school and playgroup and took them home. When Dad came back from work they had tea together, and played and talked. On Wednesdays Martha went to Cookery Club and on Fridays to Costumes Club. Every Thursday Dad played five-a-side football. And although it was not at all the same without Mum, at least they were still themselves.

Then Dad began to change. He decided he didn't like being a cinematographer, and, even though he handled the best-known television programmes and knew all sorts of famous people, he gave it up, and stopped working altogether. At the same time, they left the big old house on the hill and moved down into the suburbs, to the small house near Grandma and Grandpa. It was less expensive, and more convenient. Only a few months later Dad had an argument with Grandma and Grandpa, and they stopped picking Martha and Tug up from school and coming to tea. Dad said it didn't matter now that he was at home himself.

Then he started to behave strangely.

It was the little things they noticed first. He no longer found the time to make banana pancakes on Sunday morning, or read bedtime stories, and he was always too tired to play tennis. Before long he was too tired to take them to school in the mornings, and in the evenings he often forgot to make tea. He began to look strange too. Putting away all his smart suits and blazers, he wore nothing but old pairs of jeans and T-shirts. He went for days without shaving, and almost never brushed his hair. 'It doesn't bother me,' he said. 'I don't see why it should bother you.' Now even his voice sounded different, sometimes whispery, sometimes loud and sudden. He was no longer quiet, as he had been in the months after Mum died. He was often larky and excitable, even hilarious. He specialized in lavish surprises. In the summer he hired a pink stretch limousine to take them to the opening night of a new movie in town (though when they got there they found it was the wrong day). And at Christmas he bought a spectacular display of lights for the front of the house featuring three snowmen, six reindeer, a

Santa Claus and thirty-two elves (but he must have put it up wrong because it fell off into the street and broke).

It was as if he had become a different person.

What should I do about Dad? Martha asked herself. *What would Mum do?*

I must do something, she thought. *I must keep my head, and think. After all, I am eleven.*

8

*D*octor *Zhivago* is one of the world's greatest movies, Marcus said. He kindly explained it to Tug.

'Zhivago is a poet. Tonya is the daughter of a doctor. Lara is a dressmaker's daughter. Pasha is a revolutionary. Komarovsky is a fat villain.' Marcus paused for a moment. 'How wonderful to be a dressmaker's daughter,' he said, with feeling.

He went on: 'Zhivago marries Tonya. Komarovsky loves Lara. Lara marries Pasha. Then there's the Russian Revolution.'

'Why?' Tug asked.

'Because, little Tug, they're in Russia.'

Tug thought about that. 'What do they eat in Russia?' he asked, after a moment.

'I'm not sure. Bears, I think.'

'How wonderful to eat bears,' Tug said, with feeling.

Marcus went on: 'It's very snowy in Russia. Zhivago falls in love with Lara in the snow. Tonya lives alone in the snow. Zhivago goes back to Tonya.'

Tug nodded thoughtfully.

'Because of the snow Pasha goes mad. Zhivago goes back to Lara. Lara leaves with Komarovsky. Zhivago dies. Pretty straightforward, isn't it?' He coughed modestly. 'Martha?'

'Yes?'

'Is my hat ready?'

Martha produced an enormous fur object, and Marcus took it from her with delight. 'Feel it,' he said. 'Feel how soft it is. You see, little Tug, it's all to do with snow. Now, do you have any questions?'

'Yes.'

'Excellent. You are an attentive and intelligent boy. What is your question?'

'What do bears taste of?'

When they had finished recording for the afternoon, Martha asked Marcus for his advice.

'Certainly. Is it to do with the film?'

'No. It's about something else.' She felt nervous, and didn't know quite what to say.

'Another project?'

'In a way.'

Marcus looked intrigued. 'What sort of project?'

'Actually, it's to do with helping my dad.'

54

'A project to do with helping your father? Interesting. What media are we talking about? Is it film, or mime, or art installation? Or is it live performance? What category would you put it into?'

Martha said, 'The category of good deeds.'

Marcus looked dismayed. 'This is a totally new field for me.'

At last Martha explained.

'I see.' Marcus thought deeply for a long time. 'I think we should put it under "lifestyle". The most important of all the categories. Sit here. Tell me about it.'

It was the first time Martha had talked about Dad to anybody apart from Tug; she found it hard to choose the right words. 'Excitable' was one word she used. Also 'forgetful', 'careless' and 'moody'. She described how tired Dad was when he wasn't larky, and listed his recent ailments, and mentioned that he had fallen off the front of the house. She did not say that he was strange. She did not know what 'strange' meant to Marcus.

'Sometimes,' she said, 'he's very funny, and he makes us all laugh, and he thinks up wonderful treats like midnight picnics. But sometimes he's sad. And lazy. And he doesn't look well. He's very white in a dirty sort of way. The truth is, I just don't understand him any more.'

'She doesn't understand me either,' Tug put in. 'She doesn't understand *being hungry*, Marcus.'

'Dear, dear,' Marcus said. 'How long has your father been like this? Since your mother died?'

'No. At first he was a bit quieter. He never ever talked about Mum, which was a bit weird, but basically he was the same as before. He started to change a few months ago, after we moved house. I don't know why.'

Marcus became thoughtful. It was a side of him they didn't often see. Usually he behaved as if he were acting – as if he were playing the role of himself in his own movie. But he had another side which he kept hidden, a kinder and slower side, and he had a certain look which went with it, puzzled and soft.

He turned his puzzled, soft face towards Martha.

'I think you should encourage him to get a job,' he said. 'He'll be happier if he's busy. And it sounds like he should work on his fitness. Fitness will make him feel more energetic. Also, calmer.'

Martha was pleased with these ideas.

'One more thing.'

'What?'

'Something I must suggest delicately.'

'What is it?'

Marcus hesitated. 'I think you should get him a girlfriend.'

'A girlfriend!' Martha was taken by surprise. The thought of welcoming a stranger into the family, even temporarily, made her anxious. She pointed her nose at Marcus, and said sharply, 'Why does he have to have a girlfriend?'

Marcus put his hand on hers. 'No one will ever replace your mother. A wonderful actress,' he added, respectfully. 'A girlfriend's just a project, something to do. With a girlfriend, your father will have to make an effort, smarten himself up, behave himself, be less careless, less forgetful. I think a girlfriend would be very stimulating for him.'

Martha thought about it. She thought about Mum, and had the sudden, surprising feeling that Mum would agree with Marcus. Mum used to say, *Always do what's best, even if you don't like it.*

She calmed down.

'All right,' she said. 'It's a good idea. Though he's so white and dirty at the moment I don't know that girl-friends will like him. He's very nice,' she added, 'but it's hard to see straight away.'

'Remember fitness. Get him to a gym, Martha. Tone him. Buff him. Dude him up. It's all to do with the project.'

Martha was impressed. 'I didn't expect you to be so practical, Marcus.'

'I aim to be unexpected,' he said modestly.

'Thank you.'

'You're welcome.' His puzzled, soft expression disappeared. 'Besides,' he said, 'I can't have my leading costume designer unhappy. What would happen to my wardrobe?'

9

B ut it turned out that Dad did not like gyms.
'Full of sinister equipment,' he said.

'What equipment?' Tug asked.

'Contraptions,' Dad said, 'for punishing people.'

They talked about jogging, which involved no
equipment, but which Dad thought was bad for
knees, and tennis, which Dad had decided some time
ago was 'boring'. Squash apparently brought on claus-
trophobia, and badminton was too slow. Golf was very
expensive and, besides, it wasn't really exercise. Tug
thought Dad might like kick-boxing, but Dad didn't.

'What about walking?' he said. 'Round the garden,
for instance. Or part of it.'

Eventually he agreed to go swimming.

It was Sunday morning; the swimming baths were
crowded with families. Mothers sat with their babies
in the baby pool, and trim elderly people did lengths
in the big pool. Kids of all ages larked in the shallows

with brightly-coloured floats. The noise of people dodging in and out of the sprinklers and jets, and plunging down the flumes into the splash pools, made echoes that banged about the ceiling. Everywhere was busy except for a section of the main pool reserved for group instruction, and the diving pool, which was closed for special training.

Dad stood on the side in his old Speedos, looking doubtful. He seemed very pale. 'Shall we go in the baby pool first?' he said.

'I'm not a baby,' Tug said.

'I wasn't thinking of you, Tug. It's warm and relaxing in the baby pool.'

Martha steered Dad to the fast lane in the big pool. 'How many lengths do you think you can do?' she asked.

Dad looked more doubtful than ever.

'Start with twenty,' she said.

'All right. How many before I can have a rest?'

'Twenty.'

'Oh, I see.'

While Dad swam, Tug went to play in the sprinklers.

'Aren't you coming in, Martha?' he called.

'In a minute.'

She wanted to keep an eye on Dad. As she watched him, she thought again about what Marcus had said. She understood that getting Dad fit would make him healthier, and getting a job would make him busier, and that having a girlfriend might make him happier. But would these things make him quieter and more sensible, the way he used to be?

Her thoughts were interrupted by a girl who hobbled over and collapsed into the seat next to her. A heavy, red-faced girl.

She writhed in her seat, hissing. 'Foot!' she gasped. 'Cramp?'

The girl nodded urgently. Her eyes bulged.

Martha took her foot and slowly bent it back, and after a moment the girl gave a sigh of relief. 'I knew I was meant to do that – my mum's a nurse – but somehow it's hard to do on your own.'

They began to talk.

'Do you like swimming?' the red-faced girl asked. She had a blunt way of speaking which was very pleasant.

'I don't mind it.'

'I hate it. Bloody water everywhere. Up the nose, in the ears. Are you here on your own?'

Martha pointed out Tug sitting under the sprinkler

catching water in his cupped hands, and Dad, who had been moved by the lifeguard out of the fast lane into the slow one, where he was swimming with a stiff and upright breast-stroke.

The girl watched for a moment. 'What's wrong with him?'

Martha was taken aback. 'What do you mean?'

'I mean, can he swim?'

'Oh. Yes. He's just not used to it. Are you here on your own?'

The girl said that she was with her mum.

'She's a good swimmer, I expect.'

'She swims five times a week. I don't know whether she's killing time or trying to pick up men. Here she is.'

A handsome woman in a red swimsuit came up to them. 'Are you OK, Laura? I saw you limping.'

'Cramp. Gone now. She helped me.'

Laura's mum smiled at Martha. 'Would you like a drink? We were just going to the café.'

'Thank you, but I have to watch my brother. And my dad.'

Laura's mum smiled again. 'Some dads definitely need watching.'

Martha wasn't sure she understood that, but adults

often said things that weren't really meant to be understood. After Laura and her mum had gone to the café she turned her attention back to the slow lane.

A minute later she realized Dad was no longer in it. She went over to the sprinklers.

'Where's Dad, Tug?'

'He went.'

'Went where?'

'He didn't tell me. He just went.'

They began to search for him. He wasn't anywhere in the big pool, and he wasn't at the flumes either.

'Where would you go if you were Dad, Tug?'

'The café,' Tug said promptly.

They went to the café.

Laura's mum called out, 'Have you lost him already?'

'Yes,' Martha said.

'Try the baby pool. It's very warm and relaxing.'

And as they walked towards it, they saw Dad slip out of the changing rooms with a furtive look on his face and sneak into the hot shallow water.

Martha told him off.

Dad explained that if the lengths he had done in the fast lane were added to the lengths he did in the slow lane, they totalled nearly twenty, or if not twenty then almost certainly more than half of twenty, or at least nearly half, though some of the lengths were admittedly not quite lengths, but most were half a length, perhaps.

Martha was still cross. 'That's rubbish,' she said.

'I know. I feel bad. But at least it's a start. What do you think, Tug?'

'I agree with you,' Tug said. 'It *is* warm.'

They lay together in the warmth, looking at the people around them and gazing beyond to the main pool, and up at the boards of the diving pool high above them. Dad didn't look as if he felt bad. He looked surprisingly perky. His eyes were shining.

'What were you doing in the changing rooms?' Martha asked.

He didn't seem to hear her. Continuing to gaze up at the diving boards, he grinned. 'Diving's exciting. Much more exciting than swimming. I could handle diving.'

'I like diving too,' Martha said. 'Those boards are too high though.'

Dad disagreed. 'It's actually easier to dive off high boards. More time to get yourself straight on the way down.'

'Can you get yourself straight on the way down, Dad?' Tug asked.

'I expect so. If I can fall off a roof into a hawthorn tree, I reckon I can dive into some water.'

Martha looked doubtful.

'It's a pity the diving pool isn't open, or I'd show you.'

Even Tug looked doubtful.

'You two are terrible. Don't you believe me?'

'It's just that you've only just got over falling off the roof,' Martha said kindly.

Dad became excitable. 'You think I can't do anything!' His eyes shone even brighter. 'Right.' He pulled himself out of the water. 'I'll ask the attendants if they'll open the pool for me.'

'Don't, Dad!' Martha cried.

But he ignored her and they watched him walk away. He walked with a sort of swagger. Occasionally he slipped, and laughed at himself.

'Listen,' Tug said. 'He's singing.'

They listened, and, through the clatter and echoes of the swimming baths, they heard the words, faint but jaunty: 'The bear went over the mountain, the bear went over the mountain . . .'

10

A memory came back to her.

After Mum died, when she was nine, Martha had been ill. For a week or more she was feverish and frequently sick. Her whole body ached and she seemed to live in her dreams, confused and exhausted. Dad looked after her. Taking time off work, he stayed at home all day, reading stories to her, cooling her forehead with a flannel, feeding her spoonfuls of soup. He was always with her; when she had nightmares he calmed her and when she was sick he comforted her. Every day he bathed her. And later, when she was stronger, he took her to the swimming baths. In the baby pool, where she was standing now with Tug, he had supported her in his arms to let the warm water soothe her, and sung to her softly, careless of other people listening around them. The words had seemed to be a sort of spell, making her better, 'The bear went over the mountain . . . to see what he could see.'

That's what she remembered. Dad's mouth close to her ear. The magic words. His soothing voice.

That was when Dad was safe. The words of the song sounded very different now. They had a mocking air, and the bear seemed foolish, and Martha knew for certain that there was nothing on the other side of the mountain but more mountain. It made her cross.

Dad turned, laughing, waved at them and walked on.

Tug pulled her arm. 'Is he going to do it, Martha?'

'No, Tug. The diving pool's closed. Why would they open it?'

'Martha?' Tug said.

'Yes?'

'He's being strange again, isn't he?'

'I don't understand,' she said. 'He was all right until just a minute ago. Now he's all excitable. I'm not sure Marcus's plan is going to work.' She frowned. 'Do you think it would help if we got him a girlfriend?'

'Where do you get girlfriends for dads?'

'I don't know.'

She sighed and pulled herself out of the baby pool. 'I'd better go and make sure he doesn't do anything silly,' she said to Tug. 'Wait here.'

By the time she was halfway there, Dad was already talking to the attendants at the diving pool. There was a chain across the entrance and a sign: DIVING POOL CLOSED. Martha could see Dad nodding and smiling as he talked to the two women.

She heard him say, 'Not too early, am I?'

He was being jokey.

The attendants were looking at him.

One of them said, 'Are you here to train?'

And Dad said, with a grin, 'Absolutely.'

Martha speeded up. But she was too late. The attendant got up out of her seat and removed the chain from across the entrance and, before Martha could reach him, Dad was inside the diving pool area and the chain was back across the entrance.

She stopped, confused.

The attendants were talking about Dad, who was already at the foot of the ladder.

'Took me by surprise,' one of them said. 'They told me he'd be coming *after* lunch.'

'Who is he?'

'From the county diving team. Apparently he's pretty good.'

The second one said, 'Doesn't look very fit to me. Bit old too.'

They both turned and scrutinized Dad, frowning, and Martha turned and hurried back to the baby pool.

'He got in!' Tug said excitedly.

'There's been a mistake,' she said, looking up at Dad.

Everyone in the baby pool was looking up at him too. Word went round that an Olympic diver had arrived to train.

Laura and her mum joined them in the baby pool.

'You didn't say your dad was a diver,' Laura said.

'He's not.'

Together they watched Dad on the ladder. He knew people were watching him. He slipped once, turned round and grinned, and pretended to slip again, and there was laughter.

He climbed up. There were three diving boards. The first was a fixed shelf about ten feet above the water, and Dad climbed past it.

Tug cheered.

'Be quiet, Tug. People will think we're with him.'

The second board was a springboard, about fifteen feet up. Here Dad stopped.

'He's going off the springboard,' Martha said.

Tug grew more and more excited. He began to splash about, and Martha apologized to Laura's mum.

'Don't worry,' she said. 'I know how hard it is looking after little ones.'

'He's easy,' Martha said. 'It's the other one that's difficult.'

They all looked up.

'I hope he knows what he's doing,' she added anxiously. 'I don't want him to hurt himself.'

As they watched, Dad looked down and gave them a wave. They waved back nervously. Several other people in the baby pool waved back too. Encouraged, Dad gave a little bow, which raised another laugh. Then he turned to the board, lifted his arms and stood there perfectly still, chin up, very poised and serious. A respectful silence fell over the baby pool.

A minute passed.

Tug said, 'Why isn't he moving, Martha?'

Martha felt anxious. 'He doesn't know what to do. I don't think he's ever even been off a springboard before.'

'How do you go off springboards?'

'I don't know. On television they run along the board. They sort of prance. I hope he doesn't try to do that.'

Dad suddenly pranced onto the board, which immediately sank under his right foot, throwing him off balance and propelling him violently forward. Whinnying with surprise, he bounded upwards, very high, and came down crookedly, left foot first, in the middle of the board just as it sprang back up again. Body buckling, he loped up once more, even higher, hands scrabbling in the air, and, now completely out of control, crashed onto the very end of the board, which sank dramatically under him, down and down – before suddenly whipping up and lobbing him out, way above the pool. There was a moment when he hung in mid-air, spread-eagled, open-mouthed and very surprised. Then he dropped with a roar of alarm twenty feet into the waiting water.

Everyone in the baby pool stared in silence.

'He *is* strange, isn't he?' Tug said thoughtfully.

It took Dad a while to return to the baby pool. By the time he had crawled out of the water, limped out of the diving arena ('I think I'll leave it for today, thanks,' he said very quietly to the attendants as he passed) and back alongside the main pool, Laura's mum had been into the changing rooms to fetch some ointment from her nurse's bag.

'It'll help with your soreness,' she said. Martha noticed that there was something odd about her face as she spoke to Dad. After a while, she realized that she was trying not to laugh.

Laura just stared.

Martha held Dad's hand. She was cross, but sorry for him too. 'Don't try to speak,' she said.

Dad wasn't sure he *could* speak. His chest, stomach and face were bright red.

Tug said, 'Why did you make that noise?'

Dad looked at him.

'That noise,' Tug said, 'when you hit the water.'

Dad found his voice, though it was quiet and a bit croaky. 'The thing is, I didn't want to hit it, Tug. But I couldn't get out of the way in time. Was it a loud bang?'

'We thought the bloody roof was falling in,' Laura said.

Dad seemed oddly pleased. 'Do you know,' he said, 'the water in this baby pool is far too hot. It's stinging my stomach. I wonder if we might be better off in the café. How about some lunch?' he said to Laura's mum. 'On us. The least we can do after all this sympathy – not to mention the ointment.'

11

Dad was in high spirits on the way home. Martha, on the other hand, was quiet.

'Are you still cross with me, Martha?' he asked, looking at her in the rear-view mirror. 'Just because my diving's a little unorthodox.'

'No,' she said. 'I've stopped being cross.'

He grinned, and went on, 'I like swimming baths. I'm glad I thought of going. I don't think much of swimming, to be honest. But you meet nice people there.' He grinned again. 'It was a good idea of yours to invite them over. When are they coming?'

'A fortnight today.' Martha looked at him thoughtfully. He was whistling, and slapping a beat on the steering wheel.

'What did you think of her, Dad?'

'Who? Olivia?' Olivia was Laura's mum.

'Yes.'

'I liked her.' He grinned again. 'I liked her very

much.' He looked at Martha in the rear-view mirror, as if expecting a response.

But Martha said nothing. She frowned to herself. In the café at the swimming pool something odd had happened. To start with, Olivia had been very friendly to Dad, giving him the ointment ('Like calamine lotion,') and telling him what to do if he woke up the next day in pain. She had laughed at his funny stories and joked with him about the boredom of swimming ('Unless someone is kind enough to entertain us with a circus move from the spring-board'), and Dad joked back. If she thought Dad was strange, it didn't seem to bother her. But as soon as Martha invited her and Laura to lunch, she suddenly became unfriendly. Not exactly unfriendly – embarrassed. She stopped making jokes, and began to make excuses. It was clear that she didn't want to come for lunch. She didn't seem to want to see Dad again. It had taken Laura a long time to persuade her to accept.

Martha sighed. It was a shame that Olivia had gone off Dad so quickly. Otherwise, perhaps she could have been his girlfriend.

Martha said, 'I think I'll invite Marcus for lunch as well. He's good at conversation.'

'I like Marcus. Is his conversation as strange as he is?'

'He's surprisingly practical.'

'That *is* strange.'

He drove on in silence for a while.

She wondered *why* Olivia had gone off Dad.

'Let's sing a song,' Dad said at last. 'We always used to sing in the car. Who knows a song about a bear?'

Tug put up his hand.

'Please,' Martha said. 'Not the bear.'

Tug began to sing, and Dad joined in. Tug sang mainly one note, and Dad sang mainly another note, neither of which was the right note.

'Please!' Martha cried out.

'If you want us to sound better,' Dad said, 'you'll have to join in.'

They sang on.

'Sing up, Martha,' Dad shouted. 'I can still hear myself.'

She looked at him laughing. He was laughing the way he used to laugh, and he looked so happy that, despite herself, she laughed too. And then she began to sing. They sang 'The Bear Went Over the Mountain' – with wild variations and excruciating harmonies – all the way home, which seemed a very long way, and when they got there they were all hoarse.

'That was terrible,' Dad said. 'Let's not do that ever again.'

They parked the car and got their things out of the boot.

'Just to be clear,' Dad said to Martha. 'You're not cross with me?'

She shook her head.

'You're a good girl,' he said. 'It's not your fault you can't sing.'

Together they went down the street to their house, and when they got there they found Grandma and Grandpa waiting outside for them, very angry.

12

Grandma and Grandpa were Mum's parents, not Dad's. Grandma was tall and sprightly, with elegant white hair and an indignant expression. Grandpa was tubby and shrewd-looking. Both of them liked to speak their minds.

As they all walked together to their house, Grandma and Grandpa spoke their minds about Dad, who had forgotten Sunday lunch even though he had been reminded several times.

'I know, I'm sorry,' he said, again. His high spirits had vanished. He looked ashamed.

'At one o'clock we telephoned,' Grandma said. 'There was no answer, of course. When it got to two o'clock we came round and naturally you weren't in. The beef's ruined,' she said. 'We shall have to make do with salad.'

'Salad for Sunday lunch,' Grandpa said. 'Wouldn't be my choice.'

'It's the thoughtlessness that makes me cross,'

Grandma went on. 'Though why I should expect anything else I don't know. Anyway, we shall have salad, and then we shall have our little talk. You haven't forgotten about that, I hope.'

Dad didn't say anything. Grandma and Grandpa walked ahead, and Dad walked behind on his own, and Martha and Tug walked at the back, holding hands.

'What's she saying, Martha?' Tug whispered.

Martha whispered back, 'Dad forgot about us going to Grandma's for lunch.'

'So will he have to talk to her?'

'Yes.'

'Will I have to talk to her?'

'Only a bit.'

They went down the street, and along the side of the park until they came to the road where Grandma and Grandpa lived. The houses in the road were all quite big, like Grandma's. They had front gardens and garages. Some gardens had rockeries with little waterfalls, and some had miniature windmills painted red or brown.

'Martha?'

'What?'

'Will there be those glass things?'

'You know there will. Grandma collects them.'

'I don't like them. They break when you touch them.'

'You're not to touch them. Grandma will be cross. If you touch them she'll talk to you.'

He began to sniff. 'I don't like Grandma talking to me,' he said.

'Shh, Tug.'

They walked on.

'I don't like salad either,' he added quietly.

They had their salad at the big table in the dining room. Along one side of the room was a large window looking out onto an immaculate lawn, and along the other was a sideboard covered with glass ornaments. These were the Swarovski crystal figurines that Grandma collected – glass teddy bears holding up glass love-hearts, and glass koala bears playing glass cellos, and dozens of tiny kittens and rocking horses, and two huge kingfishers perching on a glass branch, and, worst of all, a row of five tall glass flamingos coloured pink with elegant breakable necks.

'You aren't eating your salad, Christopher,' Grandma said. Christopher was Tug's proper name.

He carried on staring at his plate until Martha

nudged him, and then he turned to her in surprise. 'I didn't do anything,' he said in an injured voice.

'Christopher,' Grandma said. 'Salad.'

'He doesn't like salad,' Dad said.

'It's not a question of him liking it. It's good for him.'

'Does he look unhealthy to you?'

'Looks,' Grandpa said, 'can deceive.'

Dad made a noise, and they all fell silent again.

After salad they had fruit salad.

'And now,' Grandma said to Dad, 'it's time for us to talk. I suggest the children play in the garden. Martha,' she said. 'You're a sensible girl. Please make sure Christopher doesn't climb any of the trees, or go on the rockery, or in the greenhouse. And of course neither of you should go near the water feature.'

The garden was very neat, sloping down from the house past the rockery towards a line of fir trees, where the greenhouse was. Flowerbeds and ornamental trees bordered the lawn, and in the middle of the grass was a tiny fountain. Martha and Tug sat together on the lawn as far away from everything else as possible.

'Martha, I'm hungry.'

'How can you be hungry? You've had two lunches.'

'It's the salad. It's made me hungry again. Salad does that.'

Searching through her pockets, she found the biscuits that she had saved from the swimming pool café and gave them to Tug.

They sat there in silence while he ate them.

'Martha?' he said at last.

'What now?'

'I'm still hungry.'

She sighed. 'Let's play a game.'

'All right. What game?'

'Hide-and-seek.'

'All right. I'll hide.'

First he hid in the greenhouse, and then in the rockery, and finally up a tree. Then it was Martha's turn.

Leaving him crouched on the grass counting erratically in a loud, determined voice, she went up the garden to find somewhere to hide. She thought there might be a good place among the patio furniture, or along the path that went round to the front drive. But when she reached the back of the house, she suddenly heard shouting from the dining room and she stopped in alarm.

She heard Dad shout, 'No!', and the tone of his

voice took her breath away, it was so strange and loud.

She stood there very still, head cocked on one side, listening. Grandpa said something she couldn't hear. Then Grandma said, 'Everybody knows. I don't know why you don't admit it.'

Feeling afraid, Martha crept quietly along the house wall until she came to the dining room window, and peeped through a corner of it into the room.

Dad was standing up at the end of the table, and Grandma and Grandpa were sitting facing him.

'Anyone can see it, just looking at you,' Grandma said scornfully, and Martha looked at him.

She had never seen Dad like this. His face was pale, even paler than usual, and shiny, and he was glaring all round the room (though not, Martha noticed, at Grandma and Grandpa). His voice was different too, harsh and strangled.

'You're wrong,' he said with difficulty. 'You don't know what you're talking about. Anyway,' he added, 'it's nothing to do with you.'

Martha noticed how he ran his fingers through his hair, something she had never seen him do before.

'It's everything to do with our grandchildren,' Grandma said.

Now she was talking about them! Martha pressed her face against the window, not wanting to miss anything.

Dad glared. 'Leave my children out of it.'

'You're neglecting them. Endangering them, even.'

'Nonsense!'

'You leave them unattended late at night. You're not in when they arrive home from school. Your house is dirty and hazardous. Do you even feed them properly, I wonder. Do you think we'll stand by and do nothing? We've told you before. We've tried and tried to help you. We want to help you. But if you won't let us, I warn you, we will contact the Social Services.'

'My children stay with me,' Dad said, breathing heavily. Then they all began to talk angrily, and at that moment Martha was jumped on from behind by Tug shouting, 'Found you!' into her ear. Caught off-balance, she staggered forwards with him round her waist and they tottered together past the window, fell over the edge of the patio onto the grass, and lay there in a heap.

In the dining room there was sudden silence.

'That was rubbish hiding, Martha,' Tug said happily. 'I saw you straightaway.'

She pushed him off.

'What's the matter, Martha?'

'Shut up!'

'What's happened?'

'Quiet!'

Dad came hurrying round the side of the house, followed by Grandma and Grandpa, who stood together at the edge of the lawn with their arms folded, watching him.

'Get up,' Dad said, 'and come with me.'

'Will you play hide-and-seek with us, Dad?' Tug asked.

'We're going home,' Dad said.

'Just one game.'

'Now!' Dad shouted.

Tug stared, and Martha got him up and held his hand, and they followed Dad past Grandma and Grandpa and round the house to the front drive.

Tug began to sniff.

'Quiet!' Dad said without looking round. 'Keep up.' And they went down the road as fast as they could.

'Martha?' Tug sniffed, as they went.

'What?'

'Did he break something?'

'I don't know, Tug. I don't think so.'

After a while Tug said sadly, 'I think he broke something.'

Martha didn't say anything. Holding hands, they went out of Grandma and Grandpa's road towards the park, trying to keep up with Dad, who strode ahead, muttering to himself.

13

The clock with the luminous face showed 11.00 p.m. Martha sat on her bed with *Little Women* lying unread in her lap. She ought to be asleep, but she didn't feel like sleeping. She was too busy thinking about Dad.

Dad was sitting in the shed in the garden. She knew he was there because every half an hour she went onto the landing and stood on tiptoe at the high window overlooking the garden, to check.

She didn't know what *he* was thinking about.

From Tug's room came the soft rasp of snoring, and she felt lonely. Getting off the bed, she went to her bedroom window and looked out at the moon in the sky.

Like a stain, she thought sadly. *Like something someone's spilled and has to clean up.*

She felt the beginnings of a headache. But she gave herself a shake. 'I won't be sick,' she said to herself. 'Because I have to look after Tug. And I won't mope because Mum always told me that moping gets nothing done.' She sighed. 'But what shall I do?'

Standing in front of the mirror on her wardrobe door, she pointed her small nose at herself. 'What would Mum do?' she asked her reflection.

Her reflection didn't say. It gave her a narrow look, then turned on itself and disappeared.

Barefoot and dressed only in her pyjamas, Martha went down the stairs in the silence and darkness, through the kitchen and out of the back door, into the garden.

On the patio she hesitated. She was going to do something. She just didn't quite know what. She looked down the garden towards the shed, where Dad was. It was dark in the garden; the bushes down the edge were flat and black, and everything seemed nearer than it did in the daytime. Nothing stirred, and the silence was as thick as the darkness. Fear of the dark crept over her, she felt it tickling her skin like the spiders' webs that grew across the bushes, but she took a deep breath, stepped into the shadow and let it cover her completely. Feeling her way across the broken patio, she tiptoed quietly down the overgrown lawn, the grass cold on her feet.

Dad was sitting on a chair inside the shed, she

could see the shape of him through the doorway, and when she was nearly there she whispered, 'Dad?'

There was a bang, and something fell and smashed. 'Dad?'

'Martha?' he said thickly. He sounded as if he had just woken up. 'Martha?'

He made a scrabbling noise as if he were hurriedly looking for something, or tidying something away, then suddenly fell silent as she went in.

There was a smell of something, like paint.

Hunched on the broken chair, surrounded by a mess of tools and boxes and shopping bags, he lifted his face and gave her a sullen look. He was so dishevelled, with dirt in his hair and a wet streak across his chin, that for a second she couldn't speak for shock, and there was silence.

'What's the matter?' she said at last, and it sounded odd hearing herself speak to him in the darkness of the shed. It was an odd thing to say too, she realized at once, the sort of question she often asked Tug, and which Mum had asked her when she was small. Even her voice sounded strange, reminding her of Mum's, sympathetic but practical.

She didn't feel practical though. Her mouth was dry, and her skin crawled again.

Dad didn't reply.

'What are you doing out here?' she asked.

'Nothing. Thinking.'

'What are you thinking about?'

'Nothing.'

With his head bowed and his arms round his knees, he looked almost square. She didn't like him looking like that. She wanted him to get up and put his arms round her, and tell her that everything was OK. But he stayed where he was, square and sulky, like a big Tug.

'Are you angry with us?' she asked timidly.

'No!' he said. 'Not with you,' he added.

'Are you angry with Grandma and Grandpa?'

He didn't say anything to that, but muttered to himself, and suddenly she felt so sorry for him that although she was nervous and confused she went forward and hugged him.

'I'm sorry they upset you.'

At last she felt him relax.

'We had an argument,' he said gruffly.

'I know. I heard a bit of it.'

He stiffened again. 'Did you hear what they said? About me not looking after you properly?'

'Yes.'

'I hate them dragging you into it. They've never liked me. They never thought I was good enough for her.'

He began to talk fast and his voice was oddly stretchy.

'Don't, Dad,' she said, stroking his hair, 'Please, don't,' but he went on talking, so fast and stretchy that sometimes he got his words muddled up and it was hard to understand him.

'They blamed me,' he said suddenly, 'when she died.'

There was a moment's silence, then he was talking again. 'Dragging you into it,' he said. 'Upsetting you. They've no right. They're getting old,' he said. 'They get these strange ideas into their heads.'

Eventually he fell silent.

'I still don't understand,' Martha said.

Dad ignored her. He gave her a funny look. 'Did you hear anything else they said?'

'No.' She hesitated. 'Except.'

'What?'

'Something else I don't understand. What are the Social Services?'

His face hardened. 'Social Services are a part of welfare,' he said. 'If they think children are being neglected or endangered, they take them away from their parents to live elsewhere.'

Now Martha stopped stroking, and caught her breath. 'Are the Social Services going to come and take us away?'

'No, Martha.'

'But might they?'

'No. Grandma only mentioned them to scare me. You mustn't worry.'

She had a picture of someone putting her in a car and driving her away, and taking her to a place full of strangers, and she felt her heart beating fast.

'What about Tug? Will someone take Tug too?'

Dad got to his feet – nearly falling sideways in the cramped and darkened shed – and took hold of her.

'What will happen to Tug?' she cried.

Then he was comforting her. 'Hush,' he said. 'Hush. I love you. I love the little Tug. No one's going to take either of you away from me. No one. I won't let them.' He rocked her. 'I love you,' he said. 'Remember? I love you more than dads love Marthas.'

They stood together for some time, and at last she calmed down.

He cleared his throat. 'Martha?'

He sounded nervous again.

'Yes?'

'Was that all you heard Grandma and Grandpa say?'

She hesitated. There *was* something else. But she said, 'Yes, that was all,' and he let out a sigh.

Then, stepping back from her, he stared at her in amazement.

'You're not wearing anything but your pyjamas!'

She began to explain.

'Quick, get back to bed. You'll catch cold.'

'Are you coming too?'

'In a minute. I'll just tidy this mess up.'

In the doorway of the shed she turned back. 'Dad?'

'What?'

She couldn't think exactly how to say it, and she frowned.

'What?' Dad said again.

'Are we going to be all right?'

A strange look passed across his face.

'Of course we are. We're going to be better than all right.'

'Are we really?'

He put on a funny voice. 'Sweetheart, we're going to be tremendous!'

She looked doubtfully at him standing there in his

old T-shirt, ripped at the neck, and dusty jeans, with his hair sticking up and his wet chin, and his dirty hands hanging heavily at his sides.

'I'll help,' she said.

He touched her face. 'I know you will. You're a good girl. Go to bed now. Things will be better in the morning. Things are always better in the morning.'

In the garden the darkness didn't seem so dark any more. She was used to it. Halfway across the shaggy grass she paused to gaze up at the stars flickering faintly through a veil of cloud. Somewhere up there was the moon too, floating across the sky like a lost balloon. But she was too sleepy to look for it. Overwhelmed with tiredness, she went on across the patio, and, going through the back door, the last thing she heard was a clink of glass from the shed in the dimness behind her.

14

She made a list:
>   *Get up for breakfast.*
>   *Swim (twice a week).*
>   *Apply for jobs.*
>   *Haircut.*
>   *New shirt.*
>   *Remember tea!*

Dad looked startled when she gave it to him.

'It's a list for you,' she said. 'I told you I would help.'

He gazed at it, and sighed.

For several days afterwards he seemed to take his tasks seriously. Three mornings running he managed to get up early enough to give Martha and Tug breakfast before they went to school, and twice he went (unsupervised) to the swimming baths, reporting that each time he had swum twenty full lengths without stopping. Olivia had been there, he said, and had told him she was looking forward to coming round.

That was interesting. *Perhaps*, Martha thought,

Olivia will get to like Dad again, and she can be his girl-friend after all.

She liked helping Dad. She liked being busy and getting things done, even if they were hard.

The hardest thing was helping Dad apply for jobs. He didn't seem to want to be helped ('I'm not really out of work, I'm having a sabbatical'). But she was determined. She used the computer at school to collect a lot of advertisements for him to consider. Many of them were for jobs in the television industry, which she thought he would like.

He gave them back to her. 'I want a complete change,' he said.

'What sort of change?'

He looked sly. 'I don't really know.'

She collected more advertisements.

'Aren't you being just a bit bossy?' he said, when she gave them to him.

'Aren't you being just a bit lazy?' she replied. She said other things too, like, 'You'll feel better if you have a job', and 'You can't keep on lounging in the house all day'. Now that she was helping him, she was almost enjoying herself.

Eventually he gave in. On Wednesday evening he took all the advertisements into the front room, and in a little under an hour completed five separate applications: to be a Steeplejack, a Children's Entertainer, a Lifestyle Assistant, a Groomer in a pet salon, and a Psychotherapist.

'There,' he said.

'It's a lot of different sorts of jobs,' Martha said, perplexed.

'Isn't it?'

'And you like them all?'

'Absolutely.'

'And do you feel better now that you've applied for them?'

'Ecstatic.'

It was strange that he forgot to post the applications – despite Martha reminding him – but in the end Martha took them to the post office herself.

On the whole she was pleased with him. He was working his way – slowly – through her list. He was generally well-behaved. There were no midnight picnics, or unorthodox dives in swimming pools, or falling off roofs. There were no more arguments with Grandma and Grandpa, or sulking in the shed. For over a week the house had been calm.

But now that she was keeping a closer eye on him Martha noticed little things that puzzled her. Little fits of restlessness propelled him round the house, taking him from room to room with no apparent purpose. Martha would find him unexpectedly looking for something he never seemed to find under the sink, or rearranging the sheets and towels in the airing cupboard. He seemed strangely fond of the airing cupboard. He was secretive too. Several times he suddenly left the house to go on an errand, or out to the shops, reappearing hours later with no shopping and only a sketchy explanation of what he had been doing.

One night as she was lying in bed almost asleep, he came tiptoeing into her room, kissed her very gently on the cheek, and tiptoed away again; and she heard him go quietly down the stairs and out of the front door, start the car and drive away.

She kept remembering the argument at Grandma and Grandpa's house. She hadn't told Dad the truth when he asked her if there was anything else she had overheard. She had heard Grandma say: 'Anyone can see it, just looking at you.' What Grandma had meant, she didn't know. But when Martha looked at Dad she seemed to see something too.

She just didn't know what it was.

*

Towards the end of the week, Dad became preoccupied with Olivia's visit at the weekend. He had his hair cut and bought a new shirt to wear with his summer linen suit. Several times a day Martha found him in front of the mirror.

'Do you think I need another haircut, Martha?'

'You've just had one, Dad.'

'What about a new shirt?'

'That's a new shirt you're wearing.'

'Do these socks go with my jacket?'

'Dad?'

'What?'

'Are you nervous about Olivia coming?'

He always denied it. But as the week wore on he developed nervous little habits, like talking to himself. Once Martha found him standing in front of the mirror, saying to himself over and over, 'I will be good, I will be good. And everything will be OK.'

Perhaps it will, Martha thought.

15

At last the weekend arrived. On Saturday morning Martha and Tug went to the library as usual, where Tug renewed *The Very Hungry Caterpillar*, and Martha got out *The Little Princess*. In the afternoon they went shopping with Dad.

At seven o'clock in the evening Martha was sitting in the kitchen sewing lapels onto a 1940s trench coat she was making for Marcus to wear in their new speed film. Tug was in the front room gluing. He had begun by gluing matches together to make a raft so that his JCB could float in the bath, but he had discovered that gluing newspaper made it interestingly thicker, and now he was experimenting with shoelaces. Martha could hear him singing to himself. Dad was in the garden shed. If she looked out of the window she could see him through the doorway, sitting on the broken chair reading a magazine.

It was a peaceful evening, and as she sewed Martha listened to sounds from the gardens, the leafy rustling of small birds and their sudden fluting cries. A blue-bottle buzzed against the windowpane, and late sunlight came in and lay around her in a warm glow. For the first time in weeks she felt happy. She thought about Olivia coming, and what she was going to cook. Lasagne, she decided. And chocolate mousse. She had good recipes for both.

The doorbell rang, and she heard Tug go to answer it. A few moments later he came running into the kitchen.

'Martha, she's here. That lady.'

Martha dropped her needle. 'Olivia? But it's the wrong day! We told her Sunday.'

'She said she hates to be late.'

'She's not late. She's a day early. We don't have anything to give her. And I haven't had time to get Dad ready.'

'She wants to see Dad now. She called him her heart-throb.'

Martha stared at him. 'Really?'

Tug nodded solemnly. 'What's heart-throb, Martha?'

The thought came to her – wildly – that Dad and Olivia must have become much more friendly at the swimming baths.

But it was still the wrong day.

'Wait here,' she said to Tug. 'I'd better go and explain.' She put her sewing on the table, and went anxiously down the hall.

At the front door was a woman wearing a short black dress with a red leather handbag. She had lots of blonde hair and a heavily made-up face, very big, and an enormous smile. Martha had never seen her before.

As soon as she saw Martha the woman began to talk, very fast.

'Here she is, the little lady. Stop, wait there, darling. Yes, just where you are. Let me look at you. *What* a beauty. Yes, you've got his eyes, haven't you? You've got his nose too, I can see it now. Yes, and his darling little smile. May I? Are you sure? Thank you.' She came a little way down the hall, and went on again. 'Yes, I'd made up my mind to be cross with you, you naughty girl, keeping him all to yourself. I had, really. But how could I be cross with someone so pretty? Tell me that, darling. You can't. Neither can I. I don't feel cross at all, not a bit. Is he ready?'

Her voice was loud and harsh, and her laugh was harsh too.

Martha was bewildered. 'Please,' she said. 'Who are you?'

When the woman stopped smiling her whole face settled into a different shape altogether, big and stiff.

'Didn't he say? Lulu. As in Lulu. Is he in here?' She went into the front room and peered round. 'Shall I wait? You don't mind? Tell him Lulu's here, darling, and raring to go. I hate to be late.' And she sat on the sofa and crossed her legs.

Martha retreated to the kitchen and stood there, dazed.

'What's heart-throb?' Tug asked again.

'Don't ask me, Tug. I don't even know who this woman is, or why she's here. It's not the lady from the swimming pool. It's the wrong lady. Perhaps she's got the wrong house.'

'What shall we do, Martha?'

She turned to him. 'I want you to go into the front room and talk to her for a minute.'

He wasn't sure about that. 'She makes me feel unhappy,' he whispered.

'It's important,' Martha said, firmly. 'I'll go and talk to Dad.'

As Tug sidled towards the front room, she ran out of the back door and down the garden. Dad saw her coming and came out of the shed to meet her.

'What's the matter?'

'Lulu.'

'What?'

'Someone called Lulu.'

'Someone called Lulu?'

'A lady with blonde hair.'

Dad looked blank.

'And a very big face.'

'Oh no!' Dad said. 'Lulu! Not here?'

Martha nodded. 'In the front room. Who is she? Do you know her?'

Dad looked awkward. 'Well. I don't really know her. I just sort of met her.'

'Where did you meet her?'

'I'm trying to remember. I think it was in The Crooked Pot.'

'The Crooked Pot?'

'It's a bar. She's come here? I don't remember giving her my address.'

Martha was bewildered. 'You met this lady in a *bar*?'

Things were more confused than before. She tried to concentrate. 'What are you going to do? You'll have to go and talk to her.'

But Dad just stood there. 'I can't,' he said at last.

'Dad! I don't understand. What did you arrange with her?'

Dad said nothing.

'Do you like her?' she asked, more quietly. 'Is she your girlfriend?'

For a moment Dad looked as if he didn't understand the question. 'God no!' he said. 'She's too much for me. I don't know what I said to her before. I don't know what to say to her now. If she saw me . . . You don't know what she's like. I can't see her, I just can't.' He looked at her helplessly. 'Martha,' he said, 'will you explain to her?'

'Explain what?'

'That it's all a mistake.'

And with that he took a step backwards towards the safety of the shed.

In a daze, Martha went slowly back to the kitchen, where she heard Lulu in the front room saying loudly, 'Let's have the rest of the song later, shall we darling? Why don't you run along and fetch your dad for me? Tell him we'll be late, and Lulu hates being late.'

Still in a daze, Martha went down the hall.

'Here she is,' Lulu said, 'at last. Is he coming?'

When Martha didn't say anything, Lulu glared at her. 'Well?'

Her big face had a bullying look.

Martha took a deep breath and pushed all her confusing thoughts of Dad out of her mind. 'I'm sorry,' she said. 'My dad's made a mistake. He can't go out with you tonight.'

Lulu's eyes narrowed. 'What do you mean, *mistake?*'

'I'm sorry,' Martha said again. 'He hasn't been well recently,' she added.

'He was on great form last night. Listen, little girl, why don't you run back and tell him Lulu's getting a bit impatient?'

'I've just told you,' Martha began.

But Lulu got to her feet. Now her face was angry. 'I'll tell him myself then,' she said. 'Is he in the kitchen?'

Martha felt a hot flush in her cheeks. She got into the hall before Lulu and stood across it. She was breathing heavily now, and didn't say anything because she didn't know what to say, even when Lulu came right up to her. But she was determined not to move. This was *her* house, and *her* dad.

Lulu glared at her and Martha pointed her nose up at her and glared back.

'You're a proper little madam, aren't you?' Lulu said.

And at that moment Tug came roaring out of the

front room with his JCB above his head, shouting, 'She's not madam!'

Lulu stepped back hastily. 'With a dad like him, I should feel sorry for both of you,' she said, and she turned and went away in a clatter of heels, down the hall and out of the house.

Tug and Martha stood together, watching her go.

'That's a nasty woman, isn't it, Martha?' Tug commented.

Martha didn't reply. She was still breathing heavily. But her anger was fading quickly. As Lulu disappeared down the street, she suddenly seemed no more than an ordinary woman, and Martha knew that it wasn't Lulu she should be cross with.

It was Dad.

16

On Sunday morning, the day of Olivia's visit, everyone was quiet and nervous. Dad got up unexpectedly early, and came into Martha's room while she was still in bed. He was already dressed in his summer linen suit and new shirt. After standing there awkwardly for a moment, he leaned over and hugged her, and said he was sorry.

'Things are going to be better,' he said quietly. 'I promise.'

After he had gone, Martha lay staring up at the ceiling. Dad wasn't just acting strangely. He was strange. She didn't understand him any more. There were things he did – like visit bars and meet women like Lulu – that she hadn't known anything about. He was becoming someone she didn't really know. As she lay there, she remembered the night of the midnight picnic, how shocking it had been to see his face suddenly lit up strangely in the torchlight. She felt the same sort of shock now.

But someone had to keep their head. Later, she was going to be properly cross with him and make him explain everything – but not today. Today, she had to keep calm.

She got dressed quickly and went downstairs into the kitchen. There was a lot to do.

She made a timetable in her head:

Tidy the house until ten o'clock.

Make the chocolate mousse and put it in the fridge at eleven, to chill.

Make the lasagne until twelve.

Prepare the salad at twelve thirty.

Set the table.

Change into smart clothes.

Check Dad (more than once, if necessary).

Wait in the front room.

She thought that Dad would need a lot of checking, and she was right. Before she had finished chopping the onions, he had been into the kitchen four times to ask her advice about his tie, hair, choice of music and the state of his shirt cuffs.

'Dad! What's the matter with you?'

'I'm nervous. Can't I help?'

'You can't stand cooking. And you know you always make a mess.'

But he seemed very nervous indeed, and at last she felt sorry for him. For a while he stood there talking, mainly nonsense.

'It's the first time,' he said at last, in a sort of whisper.

'What do you mean?'

'The first time we've had a . . . a lady come here, since . . . you know.'

She realized what he meant. Olivia was the first lady Dad had invited home since Mum died. Remembering how excited he had been when he first met Olivia at the swimming pool, she felt sorry for him, being so nervous.

She took his hands. 'It'll be all right,' she said.

Dad still looked frightened.

'Just be yourself.'

He nodded doubtfully.

'But you can't stay here or I'll never finish lunch in time. You have to go and find something to do.'

He went off biting his lip. A little later Tug saw him searching in the airing cupboard for something, and later still Martha saw him go down the garden to the shed. At some point they both heard him upstairs talking to himself. But he didn't disturb them any more.

109

Over the next two hours Martha and Tug gradually got things done. By one o'clock, the lasagne was browning in the oven, the mousse was in glasses chilling in the fridge, the table was set (complete with flowers) and the front room was as tidy as it had ever been.

Marcus arrived first. He was wearing red-and-yellow striped jeans and a yellow string vest, and he apologized for being slightly late, saying that he had been held up by 'technical difficulties in the studio'.

'Why?' Tug said. After his initial suspicions, Tug had taken a shine to Marcus.

'A slight hitch with the equipment, little Tug. A small explosion. But we are dealing with it. Always look forward, never back.'

'Was it the camcorder that blew up?' Martha asked.

'Fortunately not.' Marcus held up the camcorder, which he had brought with him. 'No, it was another part of the house. Father says it was something to do with the fuses, though I had purposely replaced them with thicker ones to allow me to use my high-wattage studio lights.'

They went into the front room, where Tug told Marcus about his JCB nearly blowing up once. Then Dad reappeared and stood chuckling in the doorway.

It was the first time Martha had seen him in an hour, and she was surprised to find him in such a relaxed mood. He seemed to have conquered his nerves. He also seemed to have spilled something on his jacket, but from his expression he didn't mind.

'Hello, Marcus, keeping out of jail?'

'Good afternoon, Mr Luna. Yes, I stay one step ahead of the authorities.' He indicated his camcorder. 'As threatened, I've brought the rushes of our remake of *Doctor Zhivago* for you to see. I'd value your professional opinion.'

Dad, who clearly had no memory of this, or any idea of what Marcus was talking about, laughed aloud. 'You'll have to be quick,' he said. 'We've got important guests coming for lunch.' He touched the side of his nose, and winked.

'Marcus is one of them, Dad!' Martha said. 'Have you forgotten?'

Dad put his arm apologetically round Marcus. 'Marcus knows what an imbecile I am. Only,' he added in a stage whisper, 'you mustn't tell any of the others. That would be a strategic error.'

Martha looked at him. His eyes were shiny, and he was talking too fast and not very clearly.

She frowned. 'Are you all right, Dad?'

'Luckily I am.'

'You seem a bit larky.'

'Never been more serious. I'm a complete imbecile, but I've come to terms with it. Marcus here is strange. Well, OK. He deals with it. Imbecile, strange. Strange, imbecile. We don't mind, do we, Marcus?'

Even Marcus, strange as he was, seemed to find this short outburst odd. But he recovered and said politely, 'Certainly not, Mr Luna,' and began to talk to Dad about the rushes.

Ten minutes later Olivia and Laura arrived. Olivia was wearing a blue summer frock and sandals with ankle straps, and Laura was dressed in dungarees.

Dad greeted them in the hallway with a comic bow.

'Your mother's staring,' he said to Laura. 'She doesn't recognize me with my clothes on.'

Laughing loudly, he put his hand on Olivia's waist and kissed her heavily on the cheek. 'Good job I'm not wearing lipstick,' he said. 'I never wear make-up on a Sunday. Unlike Marcus, who's in the front room.'

Olivia smiled briefly and wiped her cheek.

'Dad?' Martha said. 'Can you come and help me for a minute?'

'A treat!' Dad exclaimed with mock rapture.

'Usually,' he added, 'I'm banned from the kitchen.'
He gave a wave and disappeared with Martha.

'Dad!' she whispered, when they were out of sight.
'What are you doing?'

'What do you mean?'

'Behaving like this.'

'I'm just being friendly.'

'It's too much.'

'What is?'

'The shouting and kissing, and the jokes.'

'People like that, Martha.'

'Olivia doesn't like it.'

'I bet she does really.'

'I don't like it. *Please*, Dad.'

'All right. I'll be very polite. Very quiet. You won't
know I'm here.'

And he went back out to the front room, crying,
'Drinks! Who'd like a drink?'

17

Martha's lasagne was a great success. Olivia praised it highly, Laura had four helpings (which beat even Tug), and Marcus, comparing it to a classic ballgown, called it 'a stunning piece of artistry'.

But Martha wasn't happy. From the beginning, the lunch had been spoiled by Dad's behaviour. It was as if he were trying to be a comedian, making jokes and pulling strange faces and telling funny stories. When he talked he threw his hands around, as if juggling, and no one else could get a word in. Occasionally, he excused himself from the table and disappeared from the room, only to return a few minutes later, flushed and more talkative than ever.

Several times Martha made secret signals to him, to calm down. But he took no notice. She frowned at him and even, when she thought no one else was looking, shook her head at him. But he didn't seem to see her. After all her work, he was ruining the meal, and though she continued to smile and talk and ask people if they wanted more lasagne, she grew more and more upset.

As lunch went on, she noticed how the others stopped laughing with Dad, or even responding to him. It was as if they were doing their best to pretend he wasn't there. Laura, who had an interest in technical gadgetry, began to talk to Marcus about recording and lighting systems. Tug, having finished his final helping of lasagne, left the table to go to sleep under the sideboard. Olivia talked to Martha about cookery. She seemed particularly anxious to avoid talking to Dad, Martha noticed.

'I love the flavour of your lasagne,' she said. 'Is it beef or pork?'

'Half of each. And some bacon.'

'You're a very good cook. And you're, what, only eleven?'

Martha blushed.

'I do my bit,' Dad put in, 'by keeping out of the kitchen. Generally, the further off I go the better the food is.'

Olivia smiled briefly and turned back to Martha. 'I always find with lasagne that the real problem is the pasta. Do you soak it first?'

'Blanch it. Just for a few minutes.'

'I don't know where she gets it from,' Dad interrupted again. 'I can't cook. Never could.' He laughed again, strangely loudly.

Martha made a secret signal to Dad, but he ignored her.

'I remember attempting lasagne once,' he said. 'Years ago, before Martha was born.'

Although no one showed any interest in this, he went on anyway, with great enthusiasm. Apparently one of the guests had been late to arrive for dinner, and the lasagne was over-cooked.

'Every few minutes we added water,' he said, chuckling. 'Three hours went by.'

He was being very humorous. Soon the lasagne became fantastical. He described how it had swelled up and ballooned into strange shapes, how it had hardened and thickened, and developed sedimentary layers, and how eventually it overflowed from the pan and pushed its way out of the oven on its own.

'Like a slab of living pavement,' he said.

'Oh dear,' Olivia murmured.

He talked on and on, interrupted only by his own laughter. Everyone else had stopped talking and sat looking at him, embarrassed.

'And after we had served it, no one said a word for about three minutes,' he said, sweating now with hilarity. 'Everyone just hummed politely. And then the American lady who had been late and caused all the bother said, "Well, perhaps we can build something out of it, but we sure as hell can't eat it." So we had cheese and biscuits,' he said. 'But we didn't mind. Martha's mum couldn't boil an egg. It didn't bother me. I didn't marry her for her cooking. I married her because . . .'

Suddenly he stopped talking and there was silence in the room.

Martha looked at him with horror. He had mentioned Mum.

'Dad?' she said.

He sat trembling, his mouth hanging open as if he couldn't believe what he had just said.

'I married her,' he whispered to himself, 'because I . . . because we . . .'

'Dad?' Martha whispered again, and reached out her hand to him, but he staggered to his feet and hastily went out.

No one else said anything. There was nothing to say. And when Martha looked round the table she found that everyone was staring at her, and she could see in their faces that they all felt sorry for her. Olivia took hold of her hand and squeezed it, and though, if anything, it made her more upset, Martha managed to control herself.

Because someone always has to keep their head.

She sat up straight, took a deep breath and said, in a clear, slightly quavery voice, 'More chocolate mousse anyone?'

After lunch, Olivia reluctantly agreed to stay for coffee – 'Just a very quick one!' – while Laura took a look at Marcus's camcorder. Dad had returned to the table by now and was in a different mood, quiet and shame-faced, but there was no doubt that Olivia wanted to leave as soon as possible. The lunch had been spoiled.

Upstairs in Martha's room, Marcus showed Laura his camcorder, and Laura described her even more impressive movie camera, and they swapped information about technical specifications while Martha sat quietly on her own in a corner of the room.

'It has zoom and slo-mo?' Marcus was saying. 'That's interesting. Tell me, are you using it for any particular project at the moment?'

Martha wasn't even listening to them. She was lost

in her own unhappy thoughts. Although Dad had been larky before, he had never been so out-of-control, one minute laughing like a madman, the next almost crying. Even allowing for his nervousness, he was impossible to understand. He was silly, and unhappy, and excitable, and mad, and angry, and lazy, and unfair and strange all at the same time – and she had absolutely no idea why.

After a while she realized that Marcus and Laura had stopped talking and were looking at her.

For a moment they were all silent, then Laura said, 'So, how long's your dad been drinking?'

Martha stared at her. 'Drinking?'

'Booze. Alcohol.'

Martha shook her head in confusion. 'I didn't see him drink anything.'

'He kept going out to get it.'

'But I don't think he drinks at all.'

'Probably he hides it round the house and drinks when you're not looking.'

'Even when we go shopping, he never buys drink.'

'No, he'll buy it separately, from other places, when you're not there.'

A little tremor went through Martha. 'How do you know all this?'

'Because my dad was a drunk too. That's why Mum divorced him. Your dad never stood a chance with her. She says she can do without another one.'

Martha looked at Marcus.

'I'm sorry,' he said. 'I didn't realize until I saw him today.'

'But what must I do?' Martha asked.

No one said anything.

18

The next day, after school, Martha and Tug went to the library to exchange their books. It wasn't their usual day for going to the library, but Martha insisted.

It was warm, and in the park sunshine fell in green and yellow spangles through the leaves of the trees around the boating pond. The flowerbeds were freshly filled with marigolds, and the lawns were just mown. Round the café people stood with ice creams and cups of tea, talking.

Everything seemed the same as always.

But it isn't, Martha thought. *It's all different now.*

She was paler than usual, and as she went along she rubbed her eyes. Nearly all night she had been awake, trying to think what to do. By the time morning came she had half decided to go straight to Dad and ask him if what Laura had told her was true. But Dad was too strange to talk to. In the end she left him in bed and went to school, with all her questions still unanswered. If she wanted answers she would have to find them out herself.

Tug pulled at her hand. '*Martha?*'

'What?'

'You're not listening to me, Martha. I said, where are we going on our holidays?'

She sighed. 'I don't know, Tug.'

'Shall we go to Russia?'

'I don't think so.'

'Why?'

'Russia's so far away.'

Tug thought about this for a while. 'Martha?' He pulled on her hand until she turned to him again.

'What is it now?'

'Have you ever eaten bear?'

'No.'

'Not in a pie?'

'No, Tug.'

'Not in sandwiches, Martha?'

'No, I've never eaten bear at all.'

He examined her closely. 'You're tired,' he said, as she yawned.

'I didn't have a very good sleep last night.'

'I did,' he said.

She looked down at him walking alongside her,

small and chunky, with his soft, untidy hair and his quiet, smudged face. *Whatever else I do now*, she thought, *I have to stay calm. More than ever. After all, there isn't just Dad to think about. There's Tug too.*

They reached the library and went up the steps and inside.

She did not allow Tug to renew *The Very Hungry Caterpillar* a second time. It would be good for him to choose something completely different, she said. He chose *Gobble, Gobble, Slip, Slop: A Tale of a Very Greedy Cat*.

While Tug was choosing, Martha went across to the adult section of the library to ask if she could borrow adult books on her children's membership card.

The librarian said she could. 'Up to five at a time. Is it your first time in the adult section?'

'Yes.'

'I'll come and show you how it works. Is there anything in particular you're interested in?'

'Yes,' Martha said. But she didn't say what.

Even with the librarian's help the adult section was a confusing place. It was half an hour before Martha found what she was looking for. Tug came in and played on the computers while she searched.

At last they went together to check out their books. The librarian gave Martha a long look as she stamped them.

The books were *Gobble, Gobble, Slip, Slop: A Tale of a Very Greedy Cat*, *Alcoholism: The Family Guide*, *The Truth about Alcoholism*, *Cure for Alcoholism*, *I'll Quit Tomorrow* and *Dying for a Drink*. Martha had taken some free brochures too. They were called *Alcohol Misuse*, *Getting Help* and *Liver Disease*.

'School project?' the librarian asked.

Martha nodded.

They went back across the park towards home.

For some time Tug had been looking at Martha and her pile of books with a puzzled expression, and now he turned to her. 'Martha?' he said, frowning.

'Yes, Tug?'

'What sort of bear is best to eat?'

She sat in her room with the door shut and the curtains closed, and began to read.

The first book was called *The Truth about Alcoholism* and it was written by a doctor. There were no pictures and it contained unhelpful sentences such as, 'Drinking to excess may cause an accumulation of acetaldehyde harmful to cellular proteins'.

The second book she tried was *Alcoholism: The Family Guide*. It began: 'A wide variety of alcoholism theories are based on psychological and socio-cultural variables', and she put it down, and picked up *Cure for Alcoholism*. It seemed to be mainly about God, which was puzzling.

I'll Quit Tomorrow and *Dying for a Drink* were different, but just as difficult to read. One was written by a man who worked for a newspaper, and the other was by a football player, and both were noisy, confusing books full of parties and holidays with crowds of people drinking alcohol all day, and falling into swimming pools and waking up at airports in Brazil or Iceland.

There was no one like Dad in any of these books.

The brochures were easier to read. Questions in big colourful letters headed each page – like *What is Alcohol Misuse?* and *How Do I Know if I Have a Problem?* – and there were lots of pictures in them, of people drinking, people looking ill and people with their faces on tables full of empty glasses and bottles.

But none of these people looked like Dad.

In the end she went downstairs and borrowed Dad's big dictionary, and looked up 'Alcoholic'. It said 'Suffering from alcoholism'. She looked up 'Alcoholism'. It said 'Addiction to alcohol'.

She said experimentally to herself, 'My dad is an alcoholic.' It still didn't sound quite right.

Perhaps Laura had got it wrong. After all, Martha had never seen Dad drink alcohol. But something was making him strange: Olivia had seen it in him straight away, and Martha remembered what Grandma had said to him at her house: 'Anyone can see it, just looking at you.'

Even so, she didn't quite believe it. How could she find out for certain? She still couldn't imagine asking Dad.

Then she remembered something else Laura had said.

19

After school the next day, while Dad was out, Tug found Martha searching through the piles of sheets in the airing cupboard.

'What are you doing, Martha?'

'Nothing. Go away.'

'Is it a game?'

'No.'

'Can I play?'

'No.'

Martha carried on searching and Tug watched in silence. First she stood on tiptoe to feel under all the sheets on the shelf just above the boiler, then she got on her hands and knees and hunted round the back of the boiler on the floor, among the dusty pipes. Finally she stood up and looked at the top shelf, which she couldn't reach. She sighed. 'You have to help me now, Tug.'

'All right. Why?'

'You have to sit on my shoulders, and reach up

there, and look under the sheets on the top shelf.'

'All right.'

He got on her shoulders, and, after some wobbling, began to feel under the sheets.

'Can you feel anything?'

'What thing?'

'Can you feel a bottle?'

'Yes.'

Her heart raced. 'Give it to me.'

Together, they examined it.

'What is it, Martha?'

She read out the label: 'BestValue London Dry Gin Triple Distilled.' It was nearly empty.

'Now I believe it,' she said, and suddenly in her mind she saw an image of Dad with his face on a table crowded with empty glasses in The Crooked Pot.

She groped for Tug's hand and held it hard.

He looked at her in surprise. 'It's good to keep bottles with towels, isn't it? In case they get wet.'

His eyes were big and troubled, and she wondered if her own eyes were the same. But she wasn't five. She was eleven. She was the one who had to keep her head.

'Come on,' she said. 'We have to find the others.'

In a wooden box under the sink where Dad kept

his shoe polish they found a second BestValue London Dry Gin Triple Distilled, half full. On the bookshelves in the front room, behind a copy of Jack London's *White Fang*, they found a Special Deal Dry London Gin, three-quarters full. And in Dad's sock drawer they found a Teachers Highland Cream Perfection of Old Scotch Whisky, brand new and unopened.

'That's four,' Martha said. '*Four*.'

Tug didn't like the sound of her voice. 'That's a lot, isn't it, Martha?' he said cautiously.

Martha thought for a moment. 'Wait,' she said. She went down the garden, and in a carrier bag on a shelf at the back of the shed she found a full bottle of Special Deal Dry London Gin.

'Five,' she said to Tug.

'That *is* a lot.'

Martha thought some more.

'Wait,' she said again. Taking the car key from the nail next to the front door, she went out into the street and came back a few minutes later with a half bottle of Bells Extra Special.

'In the glove compartment, behind the log book,' she said to Tug. 'That makes six. Maybe that's it. Now you have to help me carry them into the kitchen.'

'All right. Why?'

'You'll see.'

In the kitchen, they collected the bottles on the table, then Tug passed them to Martha, and one by one she poured their contents down the sink. When the bottles were empty, Martha passed them back to Tug and he lined them up, very neatly, in a row on the floor by the bin.

'It makes a noise, doesn't it, Martha? Like swallowing. It smells too,' he said happily. 'Like paint.'

It all worked well until they reached the new bottle of Teachers Highland Cream Perfection of Old Scotch Whisky. Martha couldn't get it open, the plastic wrapping round the cap was too stiff. Fetching a corkscrew from the cutlery drawer, she began to work at it, scouring the wrapper and pulling at it with her fingers, and Tug gave her advice. But they still couldn't open it. Five minutes went by while they struggled, and they were concentrating on it so hard that neither of them heard Dad come in.

'Give that to me,' he said suddenly.

The bottle fell on its side as they jumped apart, and he bent down and picked it up.

For a moment he looked as if he was going to say something, and then he looked as if he wasn't. He left

130

the kitchen carrying the bottle, and they heard him go upstairs to his room.

Tug said sadly, 'I think he wants to keep it with his socks, Martha.'

She bit her lip to stop it trembling. 'Wait here,' she said. 'I'm going to go and talk to him.'

She had no idea what she was going to say. All the way up the stairs she tried to think of something, and couldn't. She couldn't imagine what Dad was going to say to her either. Perhaps he'd say that it was all a silly mistake, that it wasn't his drink, that he'd never seen it before. Or he might tell her a funny story, the way he sometimes did, so they could both laugh about it.

But he hadn't looked very comical. He'd looked angry.

She went slowly up the stairs, her heart beating fast. On the landing, she hesitated and looked back at Tug standing at the bottom, and he solemnly waved up at her as if she were going away for a long time. Then she went on again. When she got to Dad's bedroom, she stopped and listened with her ear to the door. Inside there was no noise at all. She stayed there for a full minute until her heart slowed down. Then, taking a deep breath, she opened the door and went in, and stood silently with her back to the wall.

He was sitting on his bed with the bottle in his hands, staring at it. 'What were you doing with this?'

'Trying to open it.'

'Why?'

'So we could pour it down the sink, like the others.'

'This is none of your concern,' he said. 'Do you understand? I ought to be very cross.'

Martha didn't say anything.

'Do you understand?'

'There's six. All hidden, like Laura said.'

Dad breathed deeply. 'I don't know what Laura has said to you, but Laura knows nothing about me, or you, or any of us.'

'Her dad was a drunk.'

Dad raised his eyebrows. 'So you think I'm a drunk?'

Martha didn't say anything.

Dad pulled the top off the Teachers Highland Cream Perfection and held it out to her. 'Take it,' he said. 'Tip it down the sink. I'm not a drunk and I don't need it. Where did you find it, by the way?'

'In your sock drawer.'

'I didn't even know it was there. I recognize it: it was a present from ages ago. I must have bunged it in there when I got it and forgotten all about it.'

'There was a bottle in the airing cupboard too,' Martha said. 'And under the sink. And behind the books. And . . .'

'All right, I know. Those bottles I hid. Silly of me. Look. You're quite often in on your own, you and Tug; I didn't want to leave alcohol lying about. Especially not with Tug. You know what he's like.'

'But there were *six* bottles.'

'I believe you. But I'm telling you I had no idea. I'd have a drink and put the bottle away and forget about it. Then when I fancied another drink I'd have to buy a new bottle. I bet some of those bottles were really dusty, weren't they?'

'Yes.'

'They won't have been touched for months.'

Now she was unsure. What Dad said sounded right. But he looked uneasy.

'Dad?'

'What?'

'Were you drinking at lunch when Olivia and Laura were here?'

He bit his lip.

'Did you keep going out to get it?'

'I told you I was an imbecile. I was nervous,

133

Martha. Frightened. I wanted to make a good impression on Olivia and I thought it would help me.' He groaned. 'I know what sort of impression I made. You don't need to tell me. But I won't be making that mistake again.'

He sat on the end of his bed, running his hands through his hair and licking his lips. His face was pale and shiny.

'Listen, Martha. Things have been bad. But they're going to get better, I promise.'

He'd said that before, in the shed. He still didn't look as if he could make anything better.

'I'll help you,' she said. 'If I can,' she added.

Then he smiled and she wanted to hug him, and be hugged by him, but he stood up briskly and handed her the bottle of Teachers. 'You're a good girl, Martha. But I don't want you to get the wrong idea. I'm not a drunk. Now go and tip that stuff down the sink.'

That was on Tuesday. The next evening, Dad was an hour late picking Martha up from Cookery Club, and when he finally arrived his breath smelled odd. It was that paint-like smell again. Martha asked him if he'd had a drink and he angrily denied it.

'Listen to me now,' he said. 'We've had that

conversation already. I'm not having you accusing me of drinking all the time.'

They drove home in silence.

Over the next few days Dad spent a lot of time in the shed and Martha spent a lot of time in her room. Often Tug came in to keep her company. He lay on the carpet looking at *Gobble, Gobble, Slip, Slop: A Tale of a Very Greedy Cat*, making gobbling and slopping noises to himself, and occasionally chatting, and Martha sat next to him trying to concentrate on *Alcoholism: The Family Guide*.

'Martha! You're not listening to me!'

'Yes, I am. You said you wanted to get a cat when you're older.'

'No, Martha! I said I want to *be* a cat when I'm older.'

When she snorted, his bottom lip began to droop, and she felt sorry for him.

'It's too late, isn't it?' he said sadly.

'Poor Tug. I'll make you a cat costume instead.'

Cheered up, he came and sat with his arms round her, to help her read.

'That's a dull book, isn't it?' he said after a while. 'They forgot to put the pictures in.'

Martha agreed. It was both dull and difficult. She went on with it because she didn't know what else to do. More than ever she felt that it was no use talking to Dad. But after hours of struggling with *Alcoholism: The Family Guide*, she had found very few sentences that she understood completely. Only one of them stuck in her mind: 'If an alcoholic doesn't get better, he gets worse, and the collapse of his health is often followed by the collapse of his family.'

I need help, she thought. *But who can help me?*

20

Casablanca was Marcus's favourite movie. He had always wanted to do a speed version, he said.

'Romance, danger, self-sacrifice. What could be more like life? Martha, darling, this trench coat is superb. You're a genius.'

Martha smiled briefly. The coat had been praised at Costumes Club too; her teacher had even said she would recommend it for display at the annual Summer Exhibition.

But she wasn't thinking about the coat any more.

Turning up the collar, Marcus looked at himself in the mirror.

'Play it again, Tug,' he drawled.

'All right,' Tug said. 'Why?'

'Ignore him, Tug,' Laura said. 'He's just being strange. Pass me that clip.'

Laura was positioning her Sanyo 1010 on its revolving perch and Tug was helping her. Laura was Marcus's new first grip.

Martha didn't mind Laura taking over the camera-work. It was Laura's camera, after all. Martha was Costumes, as usual. Marcus had tried hard to persuade her to play the part of the heroine, Ilsa Lund, but Martha said she didn't like acting.

'But your mother, Martha. I'm sure you'd be a wonderful actress.'

'I'm not my mother.'

So Marcus was going to play Ilsa himself, and also Victor, her husband, and Rick the hero and various policemen. Ilsa was a Swedish beauty noted for her accent and her hats. Victor was a Czech freedom fighter with a cough. Rick had a drawl and a trench coat. And Marcus had voices for them all.

He explained the story to Tug. 'Rick loves Ilsa, but she left him for Victor. You understand?'

Tug nodded.

'And then she comes back and says she loves Rick. You see?'

Tug nodded again.

'So Rick sends her back to Victor. Got it?'

Tug said he thought that sounded all right.

Marcus was silent for a moment. 'There's a night club scene,' he said. 'I don't suppose you can play the piano?'

Tug shook his head.

'But you can sing, of course. I wonder what. It needs to be haunting, emotional. Yet uplifting, resonant with hope. And at the same time sad and poignant.'

Together, they thought about this.

'How about "The Bear Went Over the Mountain"?' Marcus said. 'That should strike the right sort of note.'

'All right,' Tug said. 'But will there be biscuits?'

They were busy all morning: Ilsa met Rick, and then Rick met Victor, and then all three met together, which required some tricky camerawork from Laura. Tug sang his song and Marcus – to his delight – had fifteen costume changes. They filmed a lot of the action in slow-motion, and quite often zoomed in. It was a cheerful, energetic session. Only Martha was quiet.

At eleven o'clock they stopped for biscuits and perched around the studio, chatting. Marcus was wearing the trench coat, high-heeled shoes and a fez, and he addressed Laura and Tug, who were partly listening, on the importance of style in the movie business.

'Though teamwork is important too,' he added generously. 'Even the greatest stars need back-up.'

He was not his usual upbeat self, however; his voice was un-Marcus-like, flatter, almost normal. He exchanged anxious glances with Laura and they both kept turning to look at Martha, who sat on the floor looking at the carpet.

Eventually the conversation died, and when Martha looked up she found Laura and Marcus watching her in silence.

Something about the silence made her eyes fill with tears.

'How many hiding places were there?' Laura asked quietly.

'Six.'

'And what did you find?' Marcus asked.

Martha told him.

He shook his head sadly. 'I can't believe BestValue gin is any good at all,' he said.

Laura asked what Martha had done with the drink and Martha told her.

'I helped,' Tug said. 'It made noises.'

'What did your dad say?'

'He said he wasn't a drunk.'

'I've heard that one before.'

Martha sat on the floor feeling helpless. 'I want to help him,' she said, 'but I don't know how. I can't

140

even talk to him. He won't listen. And he doesn't tell me the truth.'

'Team work,' Marcus said. He was looking at her with his soft, puzzled face. 'We'll come up with a plan to help you.'

'What plan?'

'I don't know yet.'

They all thought for a while.

'What about sending him to a rehab clinic?' Marcus said. 'The Priory, for instance.'

'What's a rehab clinic?'

'Where celebrities go for a rest,' Laura said. 'Very expensive.'

'I'm only being practical,' Marcus said. 'I'm surprisingly practical. Ask Martha.'

'You are. But I don't think that would work for us, Marcus. We're not celebrities.'

'What about the doctor?' Laura said.

'Dad doesn't like going to the doctor. He says the doctor doesn't do anything.'

'Not him. *You*. Ask the doctor's advice. What's he like?'

'He's nice. I don't know. I'd be nervous.'

'I'll come with you,' Marcus said. 'Keep you company. Smooth the way.'

'And Tug can stay with me,' Laura said. 'We can do some camerawork, Tug.'

'You have to watch out for him around equipment,' Marcus said. 'He's very enthusiastic.'

'He's all right,' Laura said. 'You're the one who's bonkers.'

Martha thought. 'Is that what you did for your dad, Laura? Go to the doctor?'

Laura looked away. 'It didn't matter what we did. He just carried on drinking. But my dad was an idiot.'

'Perhaps my dad's an idiot too.'

She thought some more. If Dad *was* an idiot he needed help, and if she couldn't help him, perhaps Dr Woodley could. He would give her good advice. She was only worried about getting Dad into trouble. Above all, she worried about the Social Services. The thought that they might come and take her away, and take Tug away, filled her with terror. She had to make sure Dr Woodley didn't tell them anything about Dad's drinking.

Laura nodded towards Tug, who was sitting cross-legged on the floor, finishing his sixth biscuit. 'How's your brother coping?'

Tug swallowed and said proudly, 'I mustn't worry. Martha says.'

'That's right, Tug.'

'Must you worry, Martha?'

'I don't know, Tug. But I must do *something*.'

She put her hand to her forehead and sighed. 'All right,' she said at last. 'I'll go and see Dr Woodley. I can't think of anything else.'

21

After school on Monday, Martha met Marcus in the park, and they walked together to Dr Woodley's surgery. At that time the park was quiet. The geese had come up out of the water and roamed bossily across the grass, pecking at each other and hissing at the occasional passer-by.

'I don't quite know what I'm going to say to him,' Martha said. 'I don't want to get Dad into trouble. But I think he's getting worse. Just like the book says. Shall I tell Dr Woodley the truth?'

'Don't ask me,' Marcus said. 'The truth and I are generally strangers.'

They reached the surgery.

'I know what I'll do,' she said.

In the doctor's room Martha sat on a chair, and Marcus sat on the bed, and from his desk Dr Woodley peered at them both through his steel-rimmed spectacles, first at Martha, then at Marcus.

'Hello, Martha. And you are?'

'Marcus.'

'Marcus Brown, of course. I don't see you very often.'

'I'm never ill.'

'I'm glad to hear it. So is it you, Martha, who's feeling unwell?'

Martha took a deep breath. 'No. I'd like to ask your advice, please. About . . . a friend.'

'By all means.'

'This friend has a problem.'

'Yes?'

Martha fidgeted. 'I don't know how to explain.'

'He drinks,' Marcus said.

Dr Woodley turned his gaze on Marcus. 'I see.'

'It's not me, by the way,' Marcus said as Dr Woodley continued to peer at him. 'I wouldn't drink the stuff he drinks,' Marcus added.

Dr Woodley turned back to Martha. 'Is the friend . . . an adult?'

Something in his expression made Martha think that, somehow, he already knew who it was, and at once she decided to tell the truth after all. 'It's my dad.'

Once she had said it she was scared, but Dr

Woodley smiled at her in a kind and thoughtful way.

'I see,' he said. 'And of course you're worried about him.'

'Yes.'

Dr Woodley removed his glasses and began to clean them with a small square cloth he took from his pocket. If he thought it was strange that Martha had come to tell him this he didn't show it. 'May I ask you some questions about your dad? It will help me to understand a little better.'

She nodded, nervously.

'Does he drink every day?'

'I think so.'

'And what does he drink?'

'BestValue London Dry Gin Triple Distilled. Mainly.'

Marcus tutted quietly.

Dr Woodley said, 'Do you see him drinking?'

'No. He hides the bottles and drinks when I'm not looking. There are six bottles,' she added.

'How do you know he's drinking? Is he behaving oddly?'

Martha described Dad's strangeness.

'Does he ever get angry?'

Martha thought of Dad shouting at Grandma and

146

Grandpa, and the way his face had looked, pale and furious. 'No,' she said quickly.

Dr Woodley peered at her. 'Is he ever violent, Martha?'

Martha shook her head.

'Has he ever hit you?'

'No,' she said firmly. 'He would never harm me.'

'Are you sure?'

She nodded.

Dr Woodley considered this. 'Does he admit he's drinking?'

'No.'

'So I can assume he doesn't think he has a problem and wouldn't ask for help.'

Martha nodded.

Dr Woodley sighed through his nose. 'Well, that's enough questions from me. Would you like to ask me any?'

Before she arrived, Martha had organized in her head a list of things to ask, but now she forgot them all. Instead, she said simply: 'What must I do?'

'Nothing.'

Dr Woodley turned to the computer on his desk and began to tap at the keyboard.

Martha frowned. 'But I have to do something.'

Dr Woodley said, 'You're eleven, is that right?'

'Yes.'

'And how old is your brother?'

'Five. Tug's too young. But I'm not.'

At once he turned back to her. 'It's very important you don't do anything at all. Your father must do something. For that, he probably needs help. But not your help, Martha.'

He looked at her, and Martha looked back at him.

'Is he . . . an alcoholic?'

He kept looking at her. 'I think he might be, yes. Which means that he'll be behaving in unpredictable ways, and even if he isn't a danger to others he might well be a danger to himself. It makes trying to help him very difficult. So you mustn't do it. That's our job.'

'What will you do?'

'I doubt it will be me personally. There are other people better qualified.'

A jolt of panic went through her. 'You mean the Social Services?'

Dr Woodley peered at her. 'No. I think our Alcohol Counsellors are the right people. They're part of the Health Service.'

'They're not Social Services?'

'No, Martha. But, in any case, I won't contact them just yet. First I'll talk to your dad myself.'

Her heart beat fast. 'What will you say? Will you tell him that I came to see you?'

He waited a moment, to let her calm down. 'No,' he said. 'I'll tell him the results of his blood test have arrived.'

He turned back to his computer, and began to fill in information on the screen.

In the silence she began to fret. She tried to remember exactly what Grandma and Grandpa had said about the Social Services.

'We're not neglected or endangered,' she said suddenly.

Dr Woodley carried on typing.

'Dr Woodley?' she said.

'Yes?'

He stopped typing and turned to her where she sat on the edge of her seat, and she pointed her nose at him fiercely.

'Do you *promise* not to tell the Social Services?'

For a moment she thought he was going to laugh at her. But his face was serious.

'I promise, Martha. For now, at any rate.'

He went back to typing. For several minutes the

149

only sound in the quiet room was of his fingers tapping on the keyboard.

To fill the silence Marcus said conversationally, 'Perhaps I can ask you a question, Doctor.'

'Certainly.'

'I was wondering about rehab clinics. What's your opinion of them? The Priory for instance.'

Dr Woodley chuckled. 'You've been reading too many celebrity magazines, Marcus Brown. I don't think we will need to call upon The Priory in this case.'

'I was asking out of personal interest,' Marcus said.

'Aren't you a little young to be interested in The Priory?'

'Not for now, of course. I'm thinking ahead.'

'Very practical,' Dr Woodley said dryly. 'Now, Martha.'

'Yes?'

'I have all the information I need, for the time being.' He peered at her. 'You're a sensible girl, I knew that already. That's why I'm taking everything you say very seriously. I want you to know that we'll do all we can to give your dad the help he needs. But that will be between him and us. Not between you and him. If, at any time, you feel in any way threatened by his

150

behaviour, you must get in touch with me at once. And don't worry – for whatever reason – about the Social Services.'

He shook hands with them both.

'I'll have our receptionist phone in the next day or two to set up the appointment about the blood test,' he added, as they went. 'Tell your dad to expect her call. But, remember, you're not to do anything else.'

22

It was hard not doing anything. The days went by, warm and bright, one after another, and no phone call came. One week slowly passed and another began. Every morning, before Martha went to school, she reminded Dad that the doctors' surgery might phone, and every afternoon, when she came home, she asked him if they'd called.

But they never had.

'Are you sure?'

'Of course I'm sure. Why are you so interested?'

'No reason.'

As she'd thought, Dad was getting worse – not larky, but listless and irritable. He no longer went swimming, but sat around the house, staring with a glazed look into mid-air, or hid himself away in the shed. In the evenings he nearly always slipped away for a couple of hours. His face was puffy and his eyes dull, and he was often in a bad temper.

Tug noticed. 'Martha?'

'Yes, Tug?'

'I'm bored of Dad.'

'What do you mean?'

'I'm bored of him being strange. I'm bored of not going on holiday. I'm bored of not having picnics. I'm bored of not living on a boat. And,' he said, 'there's never pie.'

Martha promised to make him one. But she was feeling just as bad. She knew by now that Dad was no longer to be trusted, and as the days went by she became suspicious about the phone call that never came. Dad didn't look as if he could be bothered to answer the phone. Some days he didn't look capable of answering the phone. Eventually she decided to take some days off school, to make sure he didn't miss the call.

Dad didn't like that. 'Keeping an eye on me?' he said sourly.

'No,' she said. But she was.

If she couldn't help him to stop drinking, at least she could help him be more like his old self. It was upsetting to see him so aimless. After she'd made breakfast for him, she would ask him what he was going to do, and if he was going to read the news-paper in the front room she sat with him, doing

153

needlework, and if he sat in the shed, she did some gardening. Sometimes she suggested they go out for a walk.

'You *are* keeping an eye on me,' he said. He was very irritated.

'It's nice to spend time together.'

She made him short lists too, to keep him occupied:

Sweep the hallway.

Do the laundry.

Repair the broken kitchen cupboard.

He ignored them. Sometimes, he ignored her. And although she watched him as closely as she could, at some point in the day she would find him gone, with just a brief note left for her on the kitchen table:

Gone to town.

Or:

Back soon.

And once:

Dear Warden, Please stop spying on me.

In general he was touchy. When he received letters from Tumble Tots Entertainment and Church Property Management Ltd., telling him his job applications had been unsuccessful, he tore them up and threw the pieces across the kitchen. And he was morose when an interview with the Pooch Smooch Social Club and Boutique ended in failure.

'It was going to bite me,' he said. 'Of course I had to give it a clip.'

Every day Martha went round the house checking his hiding places. She never found any bottles. And she never once saw him have a drink. But he looked dazed nearly all the time.

Still no phone call came. Every day when she came back from collecting Tug from school she asked him, 'Did anyone call from the surgery while I was out?'

And he always shook his head.

Then, on the Thursday evening of the second week, the phone finally rang.

A woman's voice asked for Dad. It was a quiet, professional sort of voice.

Martha said, 'He's not here at the moment, I'm afraid. Can I help?'

'Are you Martha?'

'Yes.' Her heart began to beat fast.

'I'm phoning to arrange an appointment with your father, Martha. I think he knows what it's about.'

'Yes he does!' she said, and relief made her almost shout. 'Thank you! I was starting to think something had gone wrong. It seemed like such a long time to wait.'

There was a pause. 'I don't know what you mean,' the woman said. 'We were waiting for Mr Luna to phone us, in fact. He's had our letter quite a while.'

Now Martha was confused. 'Letter? I didn't know you were going to write. Dr Woodley said you'd phone.'

'Dr who?'

'Dr Woodley. Aren't you from his surgery?'

'No.'

She didn't know what to say. Flustered, she tried to remember what Dr Woodley had said to her. 'Are you an Alcohol Counsellor then?'

'No, I'm not.'

Then suddenly she was afraid, and she held the phone very tightly, and when she spoke it was in a whisper: 'Who are you?'

There was a slight pause. 'I'm from the Social Services,' the woman said.

23

Tug found Martha on the floor near the kitchen door. She was sitting cross-legged with her arms folded, her head bent and shoulders hunched, and she was muttering to herself.

She looked square.

'What's the matter, Martha? Are you in a mood? Are you hungry?'

His voice was kind and puzzled, and Martha stopped muttering and squeezed her eyes shut. Tug didn't know what was happening, and wouldn't understand if she told him. He had never heard of the Social Services. He had no idea that anyone could take him away to live with a different family. Only she knew. And she had to keep it from him. She had to keep her head. More importantly, she had to *do* something before it was too late.

She got up. 'No,' she said. 'I don't get into moods, you know that. I was thinking. I've decided I'm not going to do nothing any more. Dr Woodley was wrong.'

'I like Dr Woodley. He doesn't mind earth.'

'I don't like him at all. He broke his promise.' She wiped her face briskly. 'Never mind. You have to help me find something.'

'All right. Why?'

'It's important.'

'Is it a game?'

'Sort of.'

'Is it another bottle?'

'No, it's a letter.'

They emptied the kitchen bin and looked through the rubbish of peelings and tins and tea bags. They sorted through the balls of paper and glued shoe laces and crayoned-on cardboard in the waste-paper baskets in the front room and the back room, and delved into the pedal bin in the bathroom with its old tubes of toothpaste and toilet-roll innards. They searched in kitchen drawers, on the tops of cupboards and behind doors. Finally, they searched in Dad's room. It was hard to search there because it was so untidy.

'Dad's room is messy,' Tug said happily. Tug liked messy rooms.

'He should clean it,' Martha said. 'I'll tell him.'

At last, under Dad's bed, they found a large pile of letters, all unopened.

As soon as she saw them Martha's heart began to race.

But she controlled herself.

'Here they are,' she said calmly.

'Why does Dad collect letters, Martha?'

'Because he's strange, Tug. Bring them into my room now. We have to sort them out.'

There were many letters which were uninteresting, from companies offering credit cards or other special deals, and some that were only moderately interesting, such as those from their schools, which requested information about Martha's recent absences or asked Dad to go in to discuss Tug's behaviour. These they took downstairs and put in the dustbin. But there were three letters that Martha kept.

The first was a handwritten note from Dr Woodley, dated a week earlier. It said:

Dear Mr Luna,

   Can we make an appointment to discuss the results of your blood test, which are just in? There are some things, in fact, which we need to talk about straight away.

   We've been trying to get you on the phone, but have failed to reach you, so I'm dropping this in.

Perhaps you are away.

Do get in touch asap.

Best,

Geoffrey Woodley (Dr)

The second was a long, typewritten letter on paper headed 'Social Services Department' and dated two weeks earlier. It was not easy to understand. It asked Dad to contact a member of the 'Children in Need' team to arrange an appointment to see them, and drew his attention to an enclosed brochure headed *What is an Assessment?* which began 'Either you, or someone else on your behalf, has asked the social services departments for help with some difficulty you are having which affects your child (or children)'.

The third was another handwritten letter, from Grandma, and was also dated a fortnight earlier. It was short:

You leave us with no option but to contact the Social Services. This we have now done. We very much regret the necessity of this, and resent the fact that you have put us in this position. Regardless of what you think about us, we trust you agree that the safety and well-being of Martha and Christopher are of the first importance.

P.S. We are not the sort of people who ever thought we would have to do this sort of thing.

Martha arranged these three letters on the carpet and thought about them, while Tug watched her gravely.

'Dad gets a lot of letters, doesn't he, Martha?' he said.

She didn't reply; she was thinking. She'd got it wrong again. Dr Woodley hadn't contacted the Social Services; Grandma and Grandpa had. Dr Woodley's receptionist had phoned and phoned, but Dad hadn't answered her calls.

'Tug,' she said, 'There are things in these letters that I can't talk to you about. You're too small. I'm sorry.'

'That's all right,' Tug said humbly. He knew he was small.

'But I'll have to talk to Dad about them when he gets back.'

'Yes, Martha.'

'Now it's time for bed. It's very late. I shouldn't have kept you up.'

'That's all right.' He thought for a minute. 'Did we have tea?'

'Yes.'

'What did we have?'

'Sausages.'

'How many sausages did I have?'

'Five. And half of one of mine.'

'That's a lot, isn't it?'

'Yes, it is.'

'All right then. I'll go to bed.'

She helped him into his pyjamas, and took him to the bathroom to clean his teeth, and then she read him a few pages from *Gobble, Gobble, Slip, Slop*.

'Good night, Martha. Is the light on?'

She put the light on. 'Yes, it's on. Good night, Tug.'

As she was going out of the door, she heard him say something, and turned back. 'What is it?'

When he spoke his voice was unusually quiet. 'Are we all right, Martha?'

Her breath caught in her throat. 'Yes, Tug. We're all right.'

'But are we *really*?'

She looked at him lying in his bed, the blunt shape of his head half-hidden under the duvet, and for a moment her lip quivered. Then she put on a cheerful voice. 'Tug,' she said. 'We're better than all right. We're tremendous.'

She heard him give a peaceful sigh and, almost before she left the room, his breathing deepened and she knew he had fallen asleep already.

24

She waited up for Dad, sitting at the kitchen table in her dressing gown. Through the window overlooking the garden, she could see the moon in the sky.

Like flint, she thought. *Like a bit of shell. Sharp enough to draw blood.*

She got up and shut the blinds. She didn't want to see the moon any more. She didn't like the way it looked.

It was 10.30 p.m., quiet and cool. She had all the lights on, not just in the kitchen, but in the hall and the front room, and upstairs too. It felt safer. On the table in front of her were the three letters she had found under Dad's bed. She studied them again, first the one from Grandma and Grandpa, then the one from Dr Woodley, then the one from the Social Services, making sure she knew what each of them meant. It was clear enough. Dr Woodley couldn't help Dad because Dad wouldn't let him. Grandma and Grandpa were too angry to help him. And the Social

Services were going to take her and Tug away so they didn't see Dad again.

She pushed away the letters, and sat there with her eyes closed and her heart beating fast.

For weeks things had been getting worse, little problems slowly getting bigger. Now, suddenly, they were too big for her to do anything about. It didn't matter that she was eleven. Like Tug, she was too small to help. There was only one person who could sort things out now. Dad.

The problem with Dad was that he didn't realize how bad things had become. Before, whenever Martha tried to explain, he just cracked a joke, or slipped away to the shed, or acted strange. Now she had to make him see how really bad it all was. The letters proved it. If she could just persuade him to read the letters, he would have to take everything much more seriously. He would have to *do* something. After all, however strange he had become, he was still an adult.

She took a deep breath and pointed her nose at the clock on the wall. It was 11.00 p.m. now, and she was sleepy. *All I have to do*, she said to herself, *is make him read the letters. I can do that.*

Then she waited quietly at the table for him to come in.

He was late. Time went by, and she got sleepier and sleepier. The kitchen clock said 11.30 p.m., and then 11.45 p.m. Finally, just before midnight, still sitting at the table, she couldn't keep her eyes open any longer. Her head fell forward, her small nose hid itself in the collar of her dressing gown and at last she fell asleep.

As she slept, she dreamed. She dreamed that she was all alone in the park, having a picnic by herself, feeling lonely. Overhead, the sky turned black and all the stars came out one by one. The moon appeared, weak and trembling like a beam of torchlight, and she was gazing up at it, wondering who had switched it on, when suddenly it turned into a shiny face. Somewhere nearby a goose honked once, very loudly, like a front door slammed shut, and she sat up with a gasp.

The clock said 2.30 a.m., and Dad was standing in the doorway of the kitchen.

He didn't say, 'Surprise!' He didn't say, 'Picnic!' He swayed and clutched the door frame.

She stared at him in terror.

His pullover was inside out, there were leaves in his hair, his face was slack and shiny and he looked at her suspiciously, as if he didn't know who she was. He didn't look like Dad at all. He looked like a stranger: a man from the street.

She couldn't speak. She couldn't take her eyes off him either, and they stared at each other in silence.

At last her voice came back, a little quavery, and she said what she had planned to say: 'I've got something to show you.'

Although he showed no sign that he had heard her, he came into the room, very carefully, like a man balancing something on his head, and sat down at the table. He had a startled, wary look, as if he didn't understand where he was.

She could smell him now. He smelled of paint and perfume and dirt.

'There,' she said, and pushed the letters across the table.

Frowning, he began to read them, and Martha watched him.

After a long time he looked up at her. His face was pale, his smile crooked. His eyes were bright and narrow. 'Bad day for mail,' he said, in a sticky voice.

'They were under your bed. You hadn't opened them.'

He stared at her. 'I was waiting,' he said at last.

'Waiting for what?'

'Waiting for a good day.' Running his hands

through his hair, he picked out some leaves and looked at them in surprise. 'All the days have been bad,' he added.

'Everything's bad. You can see that now, can't you?'

He didn't say anything.

'Dad. You have to do something.'

He slowly rubbed his face. 'I agree.'

'What are you going to do?'

'Go to bed.'

He got up and pushed the chair away, and it fell on its side.

She got up too and, though she was trembling, she stood up as straight as she could and pointed her nose at him. 'Don't go! I have to talk to you.'

Ignoring her, he began to move away, putting his arms out to keep his balance, and again he seemed like a man she didn't know, a big, shambling man stumbling around in her house. He wasn't Dad any more, he was The Stranger. Her heart began to race again, and she knew she had to say something quickly before he left. 'You're drunk,' she said.

He stopped, and slowly turned to face her. A muscle moved in his jaw.

She took a deep breath and looked him in the eye, and said, 'You're an alcoholic, aren't you?'

He didn't say anything.

'I know you are,' she went on. 'I've been reading about you. Grandma and Grandpa know you are too, and Olivia knows, and now the Social Services know as well.'

He glared at her with stranger's eyes, and her skin crawled, but she made herself go on: 'If you don't stop drinking, Dad, Tug and me will have to go and live with other people. You'll be on your own then. You won't like it on your own,' she added. 'And Tug won't. And,' she said, quietly now, 'I won't either.'

'All right,' Dad said. 'I'll stop.'

'Good. How will you stop?'

'I'll keep my mouth closed so the drink can't get in.'

Her heart sank. 'Dad, it's serious. You've seen the letters. You've got to do something.'

He stood looking at her, and his eyes were so hard and small she started to get upset, she couldn't help it. 'You've got to do something because I can't do it any more.'

'Do what?' he said.

Her voice was cracking now, and her words came out in a teary rush as she tried to think of all the things he had to do: 'You have to talk to Dr Woodley.

'And you have to say sorry to Olivia.

'And you have to see an Alcohol Counsellor.

'And you have to explain things to the Social Services.

'And be nice to Tug.

'And you have to make friends with Grandma and Grandpa.'

She paused, panting.

'Anything else?' Dad sneered.

She thought wildly in case she'd forgotten something. 'Yes. You have to tidy your room.'

Lurching sideways, he snatched a mug from the draining board and hurled it against the wall, where it exploded into bits with a crash.

Everything came to a sudden stop. She stood with her mouth open, staring at Dad, who stood there glaring back at her, and there was no sound at all in the room, not even the sound of breathing.

Then they heard feet drumming on the stairs, and Tug appeared in the doorway in his pyjamas, holding on to his hair. 'Martha!' he cried. 'I heard banging, Martha!'

He ran past Dad, and she caught him up and held him, and Dad turned away from them with a groan and lurched out of the room. They heard his clumsy steps on the stairs, and the slam of his bedroom door.

170

Tug was whimpering. 'I didn't like the banging, Martha.'

She comforted him.

'I don't like Dad banging.'

'It's OK, Tug. He's stopped banging. It's over now.'

For ten minutes they stayed in the kitchen holding each other and listening for sounds from Dad's room. It was silent. At last they went together out of the kitchen and up the stairs. Tug shrank against her as they went past Dad's door, and Martha felt herself shrink too.

'I don't like him being strange,' he whispered.

'I know you don't,' she whispered back. 'I don't like it either. But don't cry any more. We're going to be all right now.'

'Are we?'

'Yes, we are.'

'Martha?'

'What?'

'Are we going to be tremendous, Martha?'

But she didn't say anything to that, and they went quietly into his room together.

25

Friday was the last day of term before the summer holidays. Lessons ended at lunchtime, and the children came out of school and ran into the streets, to the bus stops and shops. In the park there were children everywhere, standing in gangs round the benches, chasing each other across the tennis courts, playing football on the lawns marked NO BALL GAMES, hanging round the café talking. Their laughter echoed in the tennis courts and across the lake.

Martha and Tug walked together towards the library.

'Why did it make the noise?' Tug asked again.

'Because it smashed.'

'Why did it smash?'

'Because he threw it.'

'Why did he throw it at you?'

'He didn't throw it at me, Tug. He threw it against the wall.'

'Why?'

'Because he'd been drinking. You know what that does to him. I explained it to you, didn't I?'

'It makes him strange.'

'That's right.'

'And it makes him throw mugs at people.'

Martha put her hand to her head, and closed her eyes, and breathed slowly.

At the library she exchanged her old books for three new ones – *What Social Workers Do*, *What is Social Work: Context and Perspectives* and *The Social Services Inspectorate: Who We Are and What We Do* – and Tug took out *Munch!*

The librarian gave her a funny look.

Coming out of the library, they walked back across the park towards home, going in a roundabout way across the grass to avoid the geese by the pond.

They walked slowly. Even Tug noticed how ill Martha was looking. Her pale face was paler than ever, almost white against her copper-coloured hair, her eyes were sore and her nose looked small and pinched. Twice in the morning – in English and Maths – she'd felt dizzy, and had left her lessons to lie down in the Medical Room until the dizziness passed.

'Martha?'

'Yes, Tug?'

'Will Dad throw a mug at me?'

'No, Tug. He doesn't throw mugs at people.'

'Will he throw one at my wall?'

They walked past the ornamental flowerbeds, Tug asking questions about Dad and Martha trying to ignore her headache, and when they came to the park gates they were surprised by Grandma and Grandpa, who were waiting there for them.

'Hello, Martha. Hello, Christopher. Are you well, Martha? You look pale.'

Martha forced herself to smile. 'I'm fine, thank you.'

'Grandpa and I hoped we might see you here. It's the first day of the holidays, isn't it? We've brought you some holiday spending money.'

Grandpa's smile was short and cheery, and Grandma's smile was long and white.

'We're not going on holiday,' Tug said. As he said this he moved behind Martha.

'But you can have a little spending money, anyway,' Grandma said. 'Surely?'

Tug thought about this. 'All right,' he said, and sidled out again.

Grandma kept smiling. 'It's such a beautiful day. Shall we have an ice cream together? Would you like an ice cream, Christopher?'

Tug thought he would.

Martha was doubtful.

'Please, Martha,' Tug said. 'If you don't want yours,' he added considerately, 'I don't mind having it for you.'

So they went to the café in the park. It was an old-fashioned café, with coffee machines that steamed and hissed, and trays of sweets and cakes, and tubs of different flavoured ice cream in a long glass case.

Sitting at a table in the window, away from the steam, Grandma began to talk.

She said that although they hadn't seen much of Martha and Tug recently, they thought about them a lot. They were worried about them, Grandma said. And they were worried about Dad, in a different way.

'I'm afraid you must be worried too,' she said.

'We're very bored of him,' Tug said. He would have said more, but he had just finished his Strawberry Ripple and was starting on Martha's Mint Choc Chip.

Martha didn't say anything. Despite her headache, she was thinking hard about what Grandma was saying. She knew that Grandma was angry with Dad – so angry she had written to the Social Services and told them things about him. It made her wonder what

Grandma would tell them now if she found out that Dad was getting worse.

Grandma was saying how sorry she was for Dad with all his problems which he seemed unable to solve, and how difficult it must be for him to get a new job in his current state of health, and how hard it is, in any case, to bring up children on your own, though somehow she had always known, almost from the beginning, that he would find it impossible, when the time came, to meet his responsibilities.

'No, we're not worried,' Martha said suddenly.

Grandma stopped talking and looked at her through narrowed eyes.

Martha went on, 'Tug and I were just saying how wonderful he is.'

Mint Choc Chip slid off Tug's spoon as he stared at her open-mouthed.

'He's just had a new haircut,' she said. 'And he goes swimming. And he's about to get a new job. You see,' she added, 'he doesn't neglect or endanger us. Does he, Tug?' She kicked him under the table.

'Ow, Martha.'

'Now we have to go,' she said, 'or Dad will be very worried, because he worries about us. Thank you for the ice cream. Thank you for the spending money.'

And taking hold of Tug's hand she walked quickly out of the café and into the park.

'Martha,' he said, in short gasps as he struggled to keep up, 'you kicked me.'

She didn't reply.

'And I hadn't finished your ice cream.'

But she just carried on going, pulling Tug behind her, and didn't stop until they had reached the corner of their street.

She was panting. 'Listen to me,' she said. 'This is very important. We mustn't tell Grandma and Grandpa anything bad about Dad.'

'Not about the mug?'

'No.'

'Why?'

'I can't explain, Tug. You're too small. You have to trust me.'

'All right, Martha,' he said at last. 'But you needn't have kicked me.'

She hugged him tightly until he complained, and then they walked up the street together until they came to their house.

She began to search in her school bag for the key.

'Martha?'

'Yes?'

'Are you scared of Grandma and Grandpa?'

'No,' she said. It was true: she was cross with them, and anxious about what they might say to the Social Services, but she wasn't scared of them.

'I am,' he said.

He thought for a while.

'Martha?'

'What?'

'Are you scared of Dad?'

She hesitated. She remembered what Dad had looked like the last time she'd seen him with his surly face, furious voice and staggering-about movements – like a different man, not just strange, but The Stranger. But she turned to Tug and said: 'Of course not. And you shouldn't be either.'

'I don't want Dad to throw the mug,' he said in a small voice. 'It makes me unhappy.'

He looked very small and square.

'I won't let him throw the mug,' Martha said as briskly as she could.

And at last she found the key, and they went into the house together.

26

They called for Dad, but there was no answer.

Tug said he was glad.

'He must be out,' Martha said. 'He'll have left a note.'

But there was no note.

They went into the garden, to sit in the afternoon sun. Tug had a glass of orange squash and felt better. Martha went to look in the shed, just in case Dad was there, but he wasn't. After half an hour or so they went back inside.

'What's that smell, Martha?' Tug said.

'Drains, I think. Dad keeps saying he's going to fix them but he never gets round to it.'

Following the smell, they went down the hall to the front room, and there they found Dad.

He was sprawled face-down on the carpet in his dressing gown. There was sick on the dressing gown, and on the carpet and up one of the walls. His arms were round his head, his hair was wet and one of his hands was covered in blood. He was very still. As they stood there staring at him, he suddenly made a noise like a snore, and was quiet again.

Martha took Tug into the hall, sat him on the bottom step and held him until he calmed down.

'You have to stay here, Tug, while I help Dad. And you have to try to be quiet, so I can think.'

When he was quiet, she went back into the front room, and stood there, with no idea what to do.

For a minute or more she stood there staring, her mind a blank. Then she started to feel dizzy. Suddenly she was falling, plummeting in darkness, falling so fast she couldn't breathe, and the darkness was squeezing and squeezing her tummy. She put her hands out and leaned against the wall.

'I won't be sick,' she said aloud in a fierce voice. 'I won't be sick. I *won't*!'

Slowly the light came back into the room, and she found herself slumped at the foot of the wall. She hadn't been sick, but she must have fainted.

Dad was still lying in his dressing gown on the carpet, and she got to her feet, trembling. From the hallway she heard Tug whimpering to himself. She took a deep breath.

I mustn't be sick, and I mustn't faint again, she

thought, *because now I really have to do something.*

She made a list in her head:

Try to wake him up.

Check to see how badly he has hurt himself.

Get help.

When she touched it, Dad's face was wet and sticky.

'Dad?' she said. 'Dad?'

He didn't move, but he made the snoring noise again.

She began to examine him. He had cut his right hand on broken glass, bits of which lay scattered about the carpet, and there was a bruise on his forehead as if he had fallen and hit it against something. His legs were twisted under him. Martha cleared pieces of glass from around his hand, moved his arms to his sides and untangled his legs, to make him more comfortable. His dressing gown was wet and it smelled of sick and something else, and when she tried to roll him onto his side she discovered that the carpet underneath him was wet too. Looking around, she found the jagged remains of a tumbler against the foot of the wall and an empty bottle of BestValue Triple Distilled under the easy chair.

She wondered if she should call an ambulance. But

181

she didn't know if ambulances came out to drunk people. She thought of phoning Dr Woodley, but she thought that he would tell the Social Services what had happened. She certainly couldn't phone Grandma and Grandpa.

In the end she called Laura.

'Unconscious?' Laura asked.

'Yes.'

'Has he vomited?'

'Yes. And . . .'

'Wet himself?'

'Yes. And he keeps making these funny snoring noises.'

Laura said, 'He's passed out.'

'Did your dad ever do that?'

'Lots.'

'What did you do?'

'Cleaned him up. Put him to bed. Waited for him to wake up and start drinking again. Do you want me to come over?'

But Martha didn't want her to see Dad. 'Laura?' she said.

'Yes?'

'I never asked you. What happened to your dad in the end? Did he stop drinking?'

There was a pause. 'No,' Laura said. 'He died.'

Martha sat on the step next to Tug again. He was shivering, and she held him for a while to warm him up.

'He's all right, Tug. He's asleep.'

'Why?'

'Do you remember what I said about drink?'

'Drink makes Dad strange.'

'Well, drink also makes him sleepy.'

'Does drink make his hand bleed?'

'No. He's had a little accident. He's cut it on some broken glass.'

'We mustn't worry, must we, Martha?'

'No, we mustn't.'

'What must we do?'

'First we have to wash him, and put him in some clean pyjamas.'

'Why?'

'He's had another sort of accident as well. And he's been sick. Tug?'

'Yes, Martha?'

'Although you're small, you have to help me. Dad's too heavy for me to roll on my own.'

'All right.'

'And you mustn't scream again.'

'All right.'

First they took off Dad's dressing gown and pyjamas. He lay there naked and smeary on the wet carpet, not looking like Dad at all.

Tug whispered, 'I don't like the smell, Martha. But I'm not screaming.'

'You're a good boy, Tug.'

Then they started to work.

They filled the washing-up bowl with warm, soapy water and carried it into the front room; then they went upstairs to the airing cupboard and fetched as many towels as they could find and laid them out on a dry patch of carpet. Martha soaped Dad, and wiped him all over with a flannel, taking special care with his hand. When she had finished, they rolled him across the room to the towels, which took them a long time because he was so heavy and he kept disturbing them by making sudden snoring noises. Eventually they got him where they wanted him. With another bowl of soapy water Martha cleaned him a second time, including his hair, and they dried him in the towels, and slowly rolled him again – snoring from time to time – to yet another part of the front room. There they dressed him in clean pyjamas, and Martha brushed his hair and put a cushion under his head. Finally she put some sticking-plasters on his hand.

It had taken them an hour and twenty minutes, and they were tired.

They sat on the sofa and looked at Dad lying on the carpet. He was clean and tidy but he didn't look peaceful. His face was swollen.

'Now we have to clean the carpet, Tug.'

They filled the washing-up bowl with soapy water again, and scrubbed with a scrubbing brush until the bowl of water was filled with carpet fluff. They didn't know how to dry the carpet so they left it wet, and sat down again.

'Let's open the windows, to let the smell out,' Martha said, and they opened them, and sat down for the third time, and Tug began to cry very quietly, out of tiredness mainly.

'We have to keep him warm, though,' Martha said, and they went upstairs and fetched the duvet off Dad's bed, and put it over him where he lay on the front room floor.

Tug was so tired now he couldn't stop yawning.

'In a minute I'll make tea,' Martha said. 'First, let's have a nap.'

They settled down, though for a long time Tug kept

wriggling at his end of the sofa, and Martha lay there awake, trying to think.

But she couldn't think. Instead, quite suddenly, she started to cry. It happened before she could stop it. She cried silently with her face in a cushion, stifling her sobs so Tug wouldn't hear. She cried for Dad, lying unconscious on the floor next to her, and for Tug, who was frightened and confused, and for Mum, who would have known what to do but would never be able to tell her. She sobbed in silence, heaving, with her eyes squeezed tight shut into the cushion, hating the world. She cried because she thought Dad might be going to die, and she cried because she didn't know what would happen to Tug and her if he did. And finally she cried for herself, for being eleven and not knowing anything.

She sobbed so hard and for so long that she was surprised Tug didn't notice, but he said nothing and at last he stopped wriggling, and although Martha was exhausted by then she sat up to quickly check on him before she settled down to sleep herself.

He wasn't there any more.

'Tug?'

He had gone.

She got up off the sofa and went into the kitchen, but he wasn't there.

'Tug!' she called.

Out in the garden she realized that she must have slept without knowing it because it was starting to get dark: the sky was deep grey, the shed was full of shadows, and a blackbird hidden in the darkness of a tree was singing a last song. She had another shock when she saw the kitchen clock. It was half past nine. She had been asleep for about five hours.

She stood in the hall and shouted, 'Tug!'

After a moment she thought she heard something from upstairs, and she went up the dark stairwell, listening. The landing was quiet. She couldn't hear Tug breathing in his sleep, as she usually could.

'Tug?' she whispered in the doorway of his bedroom. '*Tug?*'

'Yes, Martha?' His voice was oddly distant.

She turned on the light and saw that his bed was empty.

He came out of his wardrobe.

'What are you doing, Tug?'

'I couldn't sleep downstairs.'

'But why were you in the wardrobe?'

'So I don't hear the banging.'

'What banging?'

'In case there's any banging, Martha. With mugs.'

Martha put her face in her hands. But she controlled herself, and said, 'There isn't going to be any banging tonight. Dad's still asleep.'

Tug stayed where he was.

'Do you want to come into my bed then?'

'All right.'

But neither of them could sleep. They lay side by side, thinking of Dad downstairs.

After a while, Martha said, 'Do you remember Mum, Tug?'

'No.'

'Not even what she looked like?'

He shook his head.

'She was very pretty.'

He looked at her. 'As pretty as you, Martha?'

'Much prettier than me, Tug. She was beautiful. She had red hair and green eyes and pale skin, and when she laughed her teeth were very bright.'

'I don't remember,' Tug said sadly.

They lay in silence for a while.

Then Martha said, 'But the thing about her was that she always knew what to do.'

'Do what?'

'Anything. If you lost something, she knew where it was. If you were confused, she knew how to make things clear again. If you were upset, she knew what to say to make you happy.'

Tug thought about that.

'The problem is, Tug, Dad's not like that. He doesn't always know what to do.'

Tug thought about that too. 'I want to go back downstairs now,' he said.

'Why?'

'To be with Dad.'

'Why?'

'Because he's sad without Mum.'

They went down, and Tug took the cushions off the sofa and put them under the duvet next to Dad, and got in beside him on the floor.

'It's nice and warm, Martha.' He gravely lifted up the corner of the duvet and Martha crawled in and lay down on the carpet beside him.

'It *is* warm,' she said. She put her head on the cushions.

'Can we sleep here?' Tug asked.

'Just for a little while then,' Martha said. Tug held onto Dad's waist, and Martha held onto Tug's waist.

Dad snored once, and then there was silence.

27

She was woken by the early morning light and the hubbub of little birds in front gardens along the street. Dad and Tug were still sleeping. She got out from under the duvet and went into the kitchen to find something for breakfast. They were running low on food, but she found some bread to toast. Then she went back into the front room to tidy.

The room was dim and smelled sour. She drew back the curtains, took away the washing-up bowl and scrubbing brush, and the towels, and quietly went round the room straightening it, taking care not to disturb Dad and Tug. Getting a dustpan and brush, she swept up the last of the broken glass from around the easy chair, threw away the empty Best Value Triple Distilled and put old newspaper down on the wet patches of carpet because she had an idea it might help to dry it. All the time she worked she had a funny feeling that what she was doing was useless, but she carried on doing it anyway, because she couldn't think of anything else to do until Dad woke up. Then, glancing across at him, she saw that he was awake already, watching her in silence, with horror in his eyes.

'Martha!' he said, and his voice was unrecognizable: quavery and cracked. 'Martha!'

'Yes, Dad?'

'What have I done?'

'You passed out.'

'What have I done to you?'

She said nothing.

'Can you forgive me?'

He put his hand up to his eyes, which were filling with tears, and flinched when he touched the bruises across his forehead. 'What's happened to me?' he said, in the same broken voice. And then: 'What's going to happen?'

When he was back in his own bed, he fell asleep again straight away, and slept all day and all night, and didn't wake up again until Sunday morning.

28

She made lists:

Hoover the carpet.

Clean the windows.

Throw away everything under the bed.

All the first day she cleaned and tidied his room while he lay in bed dozing or watching her. Occasionally he put out a hand for her to hold, and she squeezed it and carried on with what she was doing. Once he wept. Again and again he told her he loved her. 'You and the little Tug,' he said.

Take him tea and toast for breakfast.

Make soup for lunch, with plenty of vegetables.

For supper something light and easily digestible, like fish pie or salad and an omelette.

At first the food made him sick, and he mainly drank tea. Gradually, though, his stomach got stronger and he could manage small meals. The swelling in his face went down, the shadows went out of it, and the light came back into his eyes.

Stop him being an alcoholic.

Make him like he was before.

Make us a family again.

Make us happy.

Martha had no idea how to do these things yet, so she concentrated on cleaning and cooking.

There was just one more thing on her list:

Don't tell anyone.

After thinking about it carefully, she had decided not to tell Dr Woodley – or anyone else – about what had happened. She didn't want the Social Services, or Grandma and Grandpa, or anyone else, to find out more than they already knew. Instead, she was going to nurse Dad herself, in secret. She could do that. She had to.

After a couple of days Dad felt well enough to get up. He tottered round the house like an old man, went back to bed after twenty minutes and slept for three hours.

The next day he was strong enough to go out into the garden; and the day after that to the park. By the end of the week he was looking more like his old self: the bruising on his forehead had disappeared and the cuts on his hand were healed. But Martha noticed that sometimes his voice trembled when he talked, and he always held onto their hands very tightly when they walked together in the street.

They still hadn't talked properly about what had happened, and Dad couldn't remember. Early Sunday morning, more than a week after his collapse, Tug and Martha sat on his bed and finally told him what they had done when they found him. Martha was shy about it. It seemed easier for Tug.

'We rolled you,' he said. 'And washed you. And rolled you again. Martha helped me, didn't you, Martha?'

She nodded.

'You'd wee'd in your pyjamas,' Tug added. 'And you'd sicked yourself. But I was still quiet.'

Dad lay back on the pillows holding their hands, listening. Generally he was silent; occasionally he groaned. He looked very different now. His face was thinner and greyish, his eyes were quiet but anxious. The wild-eyed, shiny-faced Stranger had gone, and, miraculously, Dad was back again, paler and weaker, but Dad nonetheless.

'I nearly wrecked everything,' he said. He squeezed Martha's hand. 'You saved me. I didn't deserve it. Now, I promise you, things really are going to be different.'

Every morning the following week he got up early and made breakfast for them all. After showering, he would put on one of his smart suits and spend the rest of the morning on the telephone, talking to old colleagues in the television industry and making plans for meetings. In the afternoons they went out together, to play in the park, or to the shops, or for a walk along the canal. Twice they had picnics, and three times Martha cooked pie.

In the evenings, after Tug had gone to bed, Dad and Martha often sat in the kitchen with a cup of tea, talking. Dad was calm and careful. He said he was happy too, though every so often a look of sadness came over his face. Once or twice he talked about Mum, something he had never done before.

'Do you miss her very much?' Martha asked.

Their eyes met and he looked away, and nodded.

Martha thought. 'Can I ask you something?'

'Of course.'

'Is that why you drank?'

None of the books or brochures she had read explained *why* people drank.

Now Dad thought. He frowned. 'No,' he said at last.

'Then why? I don't understand.'

195

'Neither do I.'

After a while he said, 'Do you remember that time in the diving pool?'

'Yes.'

'It was like that.'

'What do you mean?'

'I didn't want to hit the water, but I couldn't get out of the way in time.'

For a while he was quiet. 'It's over now,' he said at last. 'I've been to a terrible place, and I'm never going back there. Thanks to you, we're going to be all right. Really all right. I promise. Now we can begin again.'

They had a meeting over tea. Dad hosted it, but Martha cooked the food, and Tug said he was in charge.

Dad had a pad of paper. He said, 'The purpose of this meeting is to decide the future. Because in the future things are going to be different. It's very simple. We each say what we want. I'll write it down. Then we try to make it happen. Tug, you go first. What do you want?'

It was odd how such a simple question could appear so hard.

'I'll help you,' Dad said, after a while. 'Think of little things first. Like . . . pies.'

'What pies?' Tug said at once.

'Whatever pies you like.'

Tug thought hard for several minutes.

'Come on, Tug.'

'I can't decide,' he said at last, getting upset. 'Steak and kidney is my favourite. But I *like* mince and onion.'

'Yes, but you can have both.'

Tug considered this. 'I might be sick. Can't I have half of each?'

Dad tried to explain again. 'I'm just going to write down *Pies*, Tug. That means that in the future you want a pie for tea from time to time. OK?'

'But when?' he said.

'Martha will explain later. Let's move on. Martha?'

'How about going on holiday?'

'Good.' Dad wrote it down. 'Very important.'

'How about going on more picnics?' Tug said.

Dad wrote it down. 'Now we're getting some-where.'

Dad's list started to grow.

After a while, Dad said, 'OK. That's all good. Now what about things that take longer to happen?'

'Like what?'

'Well. This house is a bit small.'

'A bigger house?' Martha said.

'Why not? If that's what you want. Once I get a new job we'll be able to afford it.'

'With a play den?' Tug asked. 'I didn't know we could ask for play dens.'

The list grew longer.

'What about you, Dad?' Martha asked. 'You haven't said anything yet.'

'This isn't about me.'

'But you said we should all choose something.'

Dad thought for a moment. 'All right. This is what I want. I want to get up early enough to take you both to school again after the summer holidays.'

They all thought about that.

'Is that it?' Tug said.

Martha said, 'I like it.'

'But will you shave and put proper clothes on?' Tug asked.

'I promise.'

'All right then. You can write it down.'

In this way the list got very long, and when they had finished it, Dad pinned it up in the kitchen, next to the calendar, so they could all see it.

Over the next few days Martha often stopped to look at the list. She was very pleased with it. It was so much happier than the lists she was used to writing herself, and real too, like the future just waiting to happen. At the same time, somehow, it made her feel sad too, she didn't know why.

Several days went by before she realized that it described almost exactly what their life was like before Mum died.

29

July ended and August began in a blaze of sunshine. Now that it was the holiday season everything slowed down. People wore shorts or sundresses and sauntered along the streets as if they had nothing better to do, or strolled into the park and lay on the grass, and fell asleep in the middle of the afternoon with newspapers over their faces. The café put its tables and chairs outside so people could sit in the sun, and on Friday nights there was an open-air film on a screen set up among the trees. A fun fair arrived on the waste ground by the canal, and for three days everything smelled of candy floss.

Laura went on holiday for a fortnight, Marcus went to do work experience at a fashion magazine called *Catwalk Crazy!* and Tug played football every day at a soccer school. Martha and Dad spent a lot of time with each other. If he was working at home, they had lunch together. If he went into town for a meeting, she went with him so that they could go to a café afterwards. Although he still hadn't got a full-time job, he had taken on some short-term projects and was hopeful of getting a proper job soon.

He was hopeful in general. Cheerful too. He met Dr Woodley for a consultation and was given the contact details for a number of agencies in case he needed help in the future. He also telephoned the Social Services, to explain things. One afternoon he even went to talk to Grandma and Grandpa. They were unfriendly, he reported, but at least they acknowledged the change he had made, and he hoped that later they might all be able to get on together.

By the middle of the summer holidays he was making jokes about the 'dark days' of the past. Remembering what he had looked like when he lay on the carpet in his dirty dressing gown, or when he snatched up the mug and threw it against the kitchen wall, Martha could hardly believe he was the same person, he had changed so much.

In the evenings she no longer stood at the window looking out at the moon. She closed the curtains and went to bed and read her new library books, *I Capture the Castle* and *We Didn't Mean to Go to Sea*. And after Dad had turned her light off and kissed her good night, for a while she lay there quietly in the pale summer darkness, listening to the faint rasp of Tug snoring peacefully down the landing and the last songs of small sleepy birds from the bushes outside. Somehow, in the end, Dad had been right. They were all right. They were even tremendous.

In the middle of August the Costumes Club held its annual Summer Exhibition, and Martha was excited to find that her trench coat was being displayed in the 'Movie Classics' section. Marcus, who felt a strong sense of ownership in the coat, was excited too. On the opening night they met to see it. It was conven-ient because Dad and Tug were going out that evening to the cinema.

At five thirty Dad dropped her off at the Community Centre, promising to pick her up again at nine, and she went inside to find Marcus.

The Community Centre was a gloomy Victorian building with a winding stone staircase going up to a dull hall. The hall windows were small and dusty, the walls were flaking and the little stage at the end was full of props. The Costumes Club people had done their best to make it more cheerful with last year's Christmas decorations, but the bunting was faded, the pendants were creased and the displays of costumes on an assortment of racks and hangers gave the event the sad air of a jumble sale.

Marcus was wearing evening dress, a white silk scarf and a top hat.

'Martha, my love, I'm distressed. I thought it was a fashion show. Where's the catwalk? Where are the models?'

Martha explained.

He wondered out loud: 'Is this the right sort of exposure for our trench coat?'

Before they looked round they sat on stackable plastic chairs at the back of the hall with a free cup of tea and two biscuits each.

'I'm sorry you don't like the show, Marcus. You look nice in your evening dress.'

'Thank you. It's my father's. How odd to think he would have such a thing. I had to make alterations. The two-tone cuffs, you see, and the suede kipper lapels.'

'Did you do them yourself?'

'I did. As I get older, I realize how interested I am in fashion.'

They sat watching people.

After a while Marcus said, 'Everyone here is very

old, have you noticed? It's all parents and grand-parents. Where are the members of the club?'

Martha laughed. 'These are them.'

'Isn't the Costumes Club for people our age?'

'No. It's for adults. Most of them are quite elderly.'

Marcus stared at her. 'Aren't there any other young people?'

'Only me. What's the matter?'

'Martha!'

'What?'

'You're extraordinary! After all these years, I still don't know you. Every Friday evening you come and sit in a dingy hall with a lot of old-age pensioners? I had no idea.'

Martha asked him to keep his voice down. But he continued to be flabbergasted.

'You're the opposite of Laura. I've only just met Laura, and I already know everything about her. But you! You're still a complete mystery.'

Martha felt embarrassed. 'Shall we look round now?'

But Marcus would not shut up. 'Take this business with your father, for instance. Anybody else in your position would be hysterical. But you're so calm, so sensible. Nothing upsets you.'

'Let's go and find the trench coat.'

'Then there's the business with your mother.'

'What about my mother?'

'Don't be snappish. We both know that if you wanted to you could be a wonderful actress, like her. But you mysteriously refuse.'

'The truth is, I can't act.'

'Nonsense. You're acting all the time. I can see through you. The truth is, Martha, my dear, you're strange.'

Martha gasped. 'Me, strange?'

Marcus smiled to himself. 'A woman of mystery,' he murmured. 'By the way,' he added, 'how is your father?'

Martha thought carefully before she answered. 'I think he's getting better.'

'Martha, that's wonderful. Take credit. Your beautiful calm has cured him.'

Briefly he held her hand, and they smiled at one another.

'Strange girl,' he added.

Then they went round the show. The trench coat had been much admired and had received a special commendation from the judges. Marcus offered to model it on the stage to music which he had brought with him, but the organizers did not think it appropriate.

At nine o'clock he went home and Martha waited outside for Dad.

Dad was late. At first Martha waited by the roadside, then, as it grew dark, by the entrance to the Community Centre. She phoned Dad several times, but he never answered.

The street lights came on. It was a quiet part of the city and there were few people about, but every so often someone walked past, and looked at Martha standing alone in the doorway, and went on again, and she listened to their footsteps fade away into the quietness. The sky darkened quickly and the street filled with shadows.

As she waited, Martha thought about what Marcus had said. She couldn't understand it at all. Marcus was the one who was strange, everyone knew that.

I am the most ordinary eleven-year-old I know, she thought, and to reassure herself she made a list in her mind of the things she did outside school:

Cooked.

Sewed.

Looked after Tug.

Looked after Dad.

There was nothing strange about any of these things.

Still Dad didn't come.

At a quarter to ten she decided to catch the bus, but just as she began to walk down the street towards the bus stop he arrived in the car with a squeal of brakes.

'Very sorry! Got stuck in traffic on the way back from the Odeon.'

She got in the back and they set off.

The problem with Marcus, she thought, *must be that he doesn't like old people.* Otherwise, why would he keep talking about the people at Costumes Club? She liked old people herself, except perhaps Grandma and Grandpa. But that was different.

'What did you say, Dad?'

But Dad didn't answer, he just squinted at her in the rear-view mirror and carried on driving. After a moment she heard him muttering again.

'Are you talking to yourself?'

He shook his head and carried on muttering.

At once she had a feeling that something wasn't quite right.

'Dad, aren't you driving a bit fast?'

He didn't say anything.

'Dad? Where's Tug? I thought he'd be with you.'

'Fast asleep. Couldn't wake him.'

'But I thought you went to a film together. Dad?'

'What?'

'Didn't you and Tug go to see a film?'

'No. Couldn't wake him. Too tired.'

She felt her heart start to race.

'But you just said you were coming back from the Odeon.'

Dad didn't say anything.

'Dad!' she cried.

He didn't say a word, just glared at her over his shoulder, and she saw then that his eyes were glazed.

'*Dad!*'

They went round the next bend too fast. There was a van coming the other way and they swerved to avoid it. Spinning out of control, they hit a bollard, skidded back across the road and crashed head-on into the wall on the far side. It only took a few seconds. There was a wild swirl of lights and the deafening roar of the engine and tyres screaming and someone shouting.

Then nothing.

30

Later, when Martha tried to remember what had happened, it was all confused.

Of the actual crash she retained only a vague impression of being flung from side to side. What came next was clear in bits, but disorganized: she remembered an ambulance, and three or four doctors all asking her the same questions at different times, and sitting on the pavement watching Dad stand in the road to stop the traffic, and a man in green overalls talking to someone she couldn't see, and Dad being breathalysed by a policeman; but she couldn't put these memories in the right order. Things were clearer when she woke up the next morning in a hospital bed. After that, she remembered things in their proper place.

To her surprise, she was glad to be in hospital. She was tired all the time. As soon as she started to think about something bad, she would fall asleep. A nurse said it was the medicine.

It was different for Dad. Although he escaped the crash with hardly any injuries, afterwards he went to pieces.

31

The lady from the Social Services arrived on the same day that Martha came home. Her name was Alison. She had straight blonde hair held back with a slide, and wore a knee-length tweed skirt and boots.

The Social Services had fast-tracked Dad's 'assessment' as soon as the police informed them about the accident. There were a number of issues to consider, Alison said, not only the crash itself, caused by Dad's drunkenness, but the fact that Tug had been left in the house on his own, and the previous reports, received from their grandparents, detailing various other items of persistent neglect dating back several months.

By the time Martha saw her, Alison had already interviewed Dad, and when Martha was called into the front room he stayed in the kitchen with Tug, as requested.

Limping slightly, Martha went across the room,

slowly lowered herself into the easy chair and sat upright. She looked different. While she was in hospital a nurse who'd felt sorry for her had plaited her hair, and it hung now in two thick braids, like copper rope. She was pale, and pinched, and when she pointed her nose towards Alison, her whole face looked fragile.

'How are you managing?' Alison asked. 'Is it awkward?'

It was awkward. With her arm in a sling, Martha had to do everything one-handed, which made the simplest movements, like opening doors and even sitting down, unexpectedly difficult. If she forgot to keep the arm still, she felt a stabbing pain in her shoulder, and there was a grinding feeling under the splint where the collarbone was broken.

'How long do you have to keep it on?'

'Six weeks.'

'And how long were you in hospital?'

'Four days.'

They had kept her in for observation, because of the concussion.

Alison had a tape recorder with her, and she set it up on the coffee table and started recording.

'Now, Martha,' she said. 'I realize that this is very

difficult for you. I've already talked to your dad and to Christopher. And I've talked several times to your grandparents. I'm doing this because I want to find a way to help your dad with his problem. But the most important thing of all is to make sure that you and Christopher are OK. Now, how old are you, Martha?'

'Eleven.'

Alison delved into her briefcase and took out some brightly coloured cards. 'I think it would be a good idea for us to get to know each other first. Would you like to play a game with me?'

'No thank you.'

'It's a good game.'

'I don't like playing games.'

Disappointed, Alison put the cards away. 'May I ask you a few questions then?'

'No.'

There was an awkward silence in which they looked at each other. Alison seemed to be a kind and thoughtful person, and Martha felt sorry for her. But she had decided not to talk about Dad. In fact she couldn't. Even thinking about him made her feel panicky and ill.

For a while Alison tried a number of different approaches, but Martha just kept shaking her head and in the end she had to give up. She turned off the tape recorder sadly.

'Perhaps another time,' she said.

'Can I ask you a question?' Martha said.

'Of course.'

'What are you going to do about us?'

Alison thought about this while she packed her briefcase, and at last she said, 'We're going to try to do what's best for you.'

'Is that what we think is best for us, or what you think is best for us?'

Alison didn't answer that. She gathered her things and got up.

'Please don't take me away from Tug,' Martha said. 'Please don't.'

But Alison just looked at her for a moment. 'I'll see you again tomorrow,' she said as she left.

One other thing Martha remembered about the evening of the crash was Dad holding her hand. He didn't hold it like he usually did, but tightly, fiercely, as if he would never let it go. He held it while she sat on the pavement, and in the ambulance, and in the hospital. He was holding her hand when she fell asleep at night, and holding it in the morning when she woke up. He held it all the time. He hardly ever spoke to her, just held her hand so hard it hurt. That's how she knew he had gone to pieces.

Now that she was home he stayed near her whenever he could, even when Marcus and Laura called with cards and presents. He followed her round, watching her with enormous eyes. And in the evening, when she went to bed, she could hear him pacing up and down in his room.

Tug sat on her bed. 'Why did you crash, Martha?' he asked again. He could never hear the story enough, even though it always upset him.

But Martha didn't want to tell him it again. 'What did Alison say to you this morning?' she asked.

'Nothing.'

'You were with her for half an hour. She told me.'

'She didn't say anything. We played games.'

'What games?'

'Not real games. She called them games.'

'What about Dad? What did he say to you?'

'Nothing. He doesn't say anything any more.'

Martha thought about this. 'I don't think they've decided yet.'

'Decided what?'

'Decided what to do with us.'

After Tug had gone to bed Martha tried to sleep. But it was much harder to sleep at home than it had been in hospital. In the end she just lay awake, awkwardly propped up on her pillows, looking out of the window. As always, the moon was there, but very faint and sketchy against the pale sky, as if someone hadn't quite finished it, or had made a mistake and tried to correct it.

Rub it out completely, she thought. *Get rid of it.*

She didn't want to see it any more.

32

Martha was wrong, as it turned out. They *had* decided what to do with them. The next day she and Tug were informed that they were to go and live with Grandma and Grandpa.

33

Grandma and Grandpa's house was much bigger than their own, and much cleaner. It smelled clean too.

There was a vestibule in which to leave their shoes when they came in, and clear plastic mats in the carpeted hallway, to prevent stains. There was shiny linoleum on the kitchen floor, which could be washed, and a large soft rug in the living room, which was not to be stepped on. The dining room, which looked onto the garden, was light and airy, and Grandpa's study, which they were not to go into without permission, was neat and tidy. All the bathrooms smelled of Pine Fresh.

The children's rooms were next to each other upstairs, also overlooking the garden. They were neat and clean too. Tug's room had bunk beds, a wardrobe and a cupboard, and Martha's had a single bed, a long desk for working at and a stereo.

'Martha?'

'Yes?'

'Why do we have to live with Grandma and Grandpa?'

'I've told you before, Tug. Dad agreed.'

'Why did Dad agree?'

'Because the Social Services were going to take us away anyway.'

'Why?'

'Because they thought Dad might accidentally hurt us if we lived with him.'

'Why?'

'Because he's an alcoholic.'

'And it makes him strange.'

'That's it.'

'But why do we have to live with *Grandma and Grandpa*?'

Martha sighed. 'Look how nice your room is, Tug.'

'Your room's nice too, Martha.'

'I think,' Martha said, 'that we're going to be happy here.'

Tug looked at her doubtfully.

She was doubtful too. But it was a relief just to be out of their old house. She couldn't live with Dad any more. Life with Dad had come to an end with the car crash. She didn't hate him – in fact she felt sorry for him – but she couldn't trust him any more. She could hardly bring herself to even think about him. *Perhaps*, she thought sadly, *Tug and I won't be happy anywhere*. But she knew she wouldn't stop being unhappy until she could forget Dad. If they stayed at Grandma and Grandpa's long enough she might at least learn how to do that.

Tug was still looking at her anxiously. 'But, Martha.'

'What?'

'Will we have to eat salad?'

She patted him on the head with her good arm. 'There are worse things than salad, Tug.'

After they had unpacked their things, they went downstairs to have lunch with Grandma and Grandpa in the dining room.

It was worse than salad. It was five sorts of salad. Grandma called it a 'cold buffet'. Everything was in its own dish with two serving spoons.

Tug looked at Martha reproachfully.

'Help yourselves,' Grandma said. 'And when you're ready we'll have a little talk. Have some lettuce, Christopher,' she added.

They had their talk. Grandma told them that she knew how very hard it was for them. She thought that they (looking at Martha) also knew how hard it was for her and Grandpa. But she was sure (putting some celery and tomatoes on Tug's plate) that they would make it work, if they all made an effort.

'There are one or two rules which will make things easier,' she said. She told them then about taking their shoes off when they came into the house, and hanging up their coats in the vestibule cupboard, and not stepping on the rug in the front room even in their stockinged feet, and not going into Grandpa's study at all, unless he actually asked them to, and tidying their own rooms every weekend, and not going near the rockery, greenhouse, trees or water feature in the garden, and using 'please' and 'thank you', and not playing music or watching TV after tea, and going to bed promptly at seven thirty (Tug) and eight thirty (Martha), and using coasters when they put down a glass of water or cup of tea because otherwise they would get water stains on the tables. There were some other rules too.

'Do you have any questions?'

'No, Grandma,' Martha said.

'Christopher? No need to play with your cucumber, Christopher.'

Tug said shyly, 'Will we ever see Dad again?'

221

Grandma tutted. 'As I explained earlier, your father will visit every weekend. You'll see him on Sunday. In just three days' time. That's not very long to wait, is it?'

'No time at all,' Grandpa said.

Grandpa was right, because Dad turned up just as they were finishing lunch. Tug had left behind his second-best JCB, he said. He stood on the doorstep with it, white-faced and pleading, wearing an old jumper over the top of his pyjamas, and Grandma talked to him.

'We're not sure this is a good idea. Can't you keep this sort of thing until your official visit at the weekend?'

'This is his *second-best* JCB. Don't you understand? It's much too important to leave till the weekend. I want to give it to him now.'

But Grandma would not let him in and Dad caused a scene.

Martha stood with Tug at the bottom of the stairs, watching in horror from behind Grandpa. Although it upset her to see Dad again, she couldn't stop looking at him. He looked so different from before, not just sad, but hopeless. His voice was broken, and when he talked he jerked his arms as if he were in pain.

She couldn't bear it. Ignoring Grandpa, she went forward quickly to the door.

'Don't cry, Dad,' she said. 'Tug will be upset. Give me the JCB and I'll give it to him.' She put out her good arm.

He looked at her for a moment, then gave it to her and held onto her hand, crying.

He said something which she could not hear.

'What?'

'I've tidied my room,' he said between sobs.

'Please,' she said. 'You have to go now. Please.'

With a last wet look at her, he turned and went erratically down the driveway, almost running, and out into the road.

Grandma closed the door. She said, 'I think, Martha, it would be best if you left these situations to me in future. You are too young.'

'But I'm eleven.'

Grandma looked down at her thoughtfully. 'You're a sensible girl, Martha. I can talk to you frankly. We must begin with your father as we mean to go on, even if it's painful. We must be very clear, and very firm. An eleven-year-old girl, however sensible, cannot be expected to deal with her alcoholic father.'

Martha sighed. 'No, Grandma.'

'He has no doubt now that we will not tolerate waywardness. Everything will go smoothly from now on, you'll see.'

'Yes, Grandma.'

But Dad must have had some doubts because he returned the same evening.

Martha and Tug were upstairs in Martha's room, and they heard his voice at the front door, shouting. He sounded drunk.

'Oh, no,' Martha said.

Tug looked at her, his eyes wide and frightened. 'What's he saying?'

'He wants to come in and see us. But Grandma won't let him.'

'What must we do, Martha?'

'Nothing.'

Her hands were trembling, but she reached out to Tug and held him on her lap, and Tug held her, and they sat there listening to Dad making large, angry noises outside. There was some banging. From time to time they heard him shout their names. They heard Grandma threaten to call the police.

Martha's head began to hurt.

'Should we go down to see him, Martha?'

'Do you want to see him?'

'No. I want him to go.'

'So do I.'

In silence they sat very still, listening to Dad shout about them. He called Tug 'the little Tug'.

Tug began to cry. 'Make him go, Martha.'

'I can't, Tug. Grandma won't let me talk to him. Grandma will make him go.'

But it seemed that Grandma could not. After a while Dad started calling loudly for Martha. He called as if he needed her desperately, as if without her he would die, and Martha sat there, white-faced, listening to him. Tug was crying loudly now.

She started to feel dizzy. But before she could be sick she struggled to her feet and went over to the stereo by the door.

'What are you doing, Martha?'

'I'm going to put on some music, so we can't hear him any more.'

The only CD in the room was *Christmas Classics*, which Grandma and Grandpa had bought many years earlier, and Martha put on Bing Crosby singing 'I'm Dreaming of a White Christmas', and turned it up loud.

But Dad must have been shouting even louder, because they could still hear him.

'Let's sing as well,' she said desperately. 'Come on, Tug, sing with me.'

Reluctantly he joined in. They sat on the carpet holding hands, singing 'I'm Dreaming of a White Christmas' as loudly as they could.

They sang the song five times from start to finish, then there was a knock on the door and Grandma came in. She switched off the stereo and at once there was silence.

Dad had gone.

'I told you quite plainly that there was to be no music played after tea,' she said.

Martha tried to explain. 'Tug doesn't like the banging,' she began. 'And I was starting to feel . . .'

Grandma said, 'I'm sorry, Martha, but I've told you before, you must leave me to deal with these situations. I realize it is difficult. But it is not helpful for you to be involved. Or to be making distracting noises. We need to be clear and firm and plain. Now I think we must have early bedtime. There has been too much excitement. Order is what we want. Come along. Pyjamas, please.'

Martha wiped Tug's face.

'Has Dad gone for good?' he asked Grandma.

'Your father has departed,' she said, 'for the time being. So now we can get back to normal.'

They went into the bathroom separately, as Grandma instructed. The bathroom was large and clean, with a soft carpet and neat racks of fresh towels. There was a bath and a shower. There was no stool for Tug to stand on at the wash basin, but they both had a new electric toothbrush, bought for them by Grandma and Grandpa.

After she had been to the bathroom, Martha went to read Tug a story, but Grandpa was reading to him already and Grandma asked her to go straight to her room.

'But I always read to Tug.'

'There is no need. Grandpa is a very good reader.'

So Martha went to bed and tried not to feel lonely. Her bed was cool and clean, and she lay there quietly until exactly eight o'clock, when Grandma came in to switch off the light.

'This has been a difficult day, Martha. I hope tomorrow will be better.'

'Yes, Grandma.'

There was a pause, and Grandma stood there looking down at her.

'I feel sorry for you, Martha,' she said. 'You have been badly let down. It makes me angry. My ideas are very different from your father's and sometimes, perhaps, you may not appreciate them, but I want you to know that I am always doing what I think is best.'

They looked at each other.

'I think a new beginning is what you need, Martha,' she said, and she patted her once on the head. 'Good night.'

'Good night, Grandma.'

Left alone, she lay there in the darkness with her eyes open, looking round her room. The darkness here felt different from the darkness in the old house: smooth and quiet. *Grandma's right*, she thought. *It's all for the best.* Her new room and new bed were for the best. Being firm and clear and plain were for the best. Order was for the best. Grandma herself – and all her rules – was for the best. With these things, she could make a new beginning.

But she frowned as she remembered Dad at the door, his face white, his arms jerking. There would be no new beginning unless she was able to stop thinking about Dad. And how could she not think about him if he came round creating scenes all the time?

For more than an hour she lay there, staring up at the ceiling, until at last, worn out with thinking, she fell asleep.

34

During the following week – the last week of the summer holidays – Grandma and Grandpa organized plenty of things for Martha and Tug to do, to keep them busy. They visited places together: parks, museums, garden centres, sites of historical interest. One afternoon they all went to an interesting flower show.

This did not stop Dad from coming to Grandma and Grandpa's house. Plainness and firmness had not had the desired effect. He came every evening, and almost always caused a scene. Grandma, or sometimes Grandpa, dealt with him, but Martha and Tug heard him, and often saw him, as he shouted and wept at the front door, and as the days passed Martha grew paler. Several times she had the dizzy feeling. Twice she couldn't finish her tea and asked to be excused so she could go and lie down.

Late one night Dad turned up in the car, saying that he was going to drive the children home, and

Grandma called the police. A few days after that, at dinner, she spoke to Martha and Tug.

'As you know, your father has been very difficult. Several times Grandpa and I have had to alert the authorities, who have been frankly less than effective. But they have at last issued a court order prohibiting him from coming here. I'm sure you'll agree it's a relief.'

'What's a court order?' Martha asked.

Grandpa had a copy of it, and he unfolded it and searched his pockets for his glasses.

'They're on your head,' Grandma said. 'But nobody wants to hear you read it. Just tell the children what it is.'

'It's like a law. It says that he can't come here or he'll be prosecuted.'

'What's prosecuted?' Tug asked.

'Punished,' Grandma said. 'Put into prison.'

'Prison!' Martha cried.

Grandma looked stern. 'I don't wish it, Martha. But I don't see why we should put up with his nonsense any more, do you?'

Martha hung her head. 'No, Grandma.'

Then she asked if she could be excused, and went upstairs to lie down.

*

231

On the day before the new school year began, Martha and Tug were kept even busier than usual. They went into town with Grandma and Grandpa to buy things they needed for school, like pens and rulers and set squares, and picked up their new uniforms which had been ordered for them, and had haircuts. Back at the house they put everything on their beds and sorted it all out. They packed their new bags and put them in the vestibule, and made sandwiches and put their lunch boxes in the fridge. After that Grandma decided that they should both have an early night.

Before their baths, they managed to sit together for a few minutes in Martha's room.

'Do you like living here, Martha?'

'I think it's for the best, Tug. What about you?'

'It's a bit tiring.' He was thoughtful. 'And they don't really understand me yet,' he said.

'What do you mean?'

'I'm hungry all the time.'

Martha sighed. 'But it's very neat and tidy. And since the court order Dad hasn't come round.'

'It's a bit too clean. And I don't like Grandma. But,' he added brightly, 'I haven't broken anything yet.'

They had baths, and separate reading, and then it was time to turn out their lights.

Grandma stood in Martha's doorway. 'Now, at last,' she said, 'we have a chance to make a new beginning. Good night, Martha.'

'Good night, Grandma.'

For a moment, as she lay there, she thought about Dad. She was sorry for him: she didn't want him to go to jail. But she was glad he wasn't coming round any more. She didn't want to see him, or think about him either.

Very carefully, she made herself stop thinking about him. Instead, she thought of herself lying in her new bed, in her new room, in the dark. As she had said to Tug, everything was neat and tidy, even the shadows, though there weren't many of those because she had closed the curtains tightly so she wouldn't be able to see the moon. It was a safe darkness, smooth and still, and she allowed herself to lie there in the quiet and the darkness and the stillness, not thinking about anything else.

This is it, she said to herself, *this feeling now. A new beginning. At last.*

She woke suddenly, and lay there listening hard. She had a feeling that something had made a noise.

Everything was quiet. She looked at her bedside

clock. The luminous face said 02.30. She sat up to listen better and the whole house was as still and peaceful as before. There was only the faint noise of rain against the window.

Perhaps it was thunder, she thought. But as she lay back down, she heard it again, a sharp, scrappy noise somewhere close.

'Tug?' she said.

She put on the lamp and got out of bed. She tiptoed to the door and opened it. The landing was dark and empty. Then the noise came again, from behind her, and she realized it was coming from the window. Going across the room, she drew back the curtains and moonlight flooded in through the rain-streaked pane. Dimly, she could see something moving in the garden below, a long dark shape swaying from side to side. It swung through the air towards her and thumped against the window, and she saw that it was a ladder.

Oh no, she thought. *Please no.*

Dad's face appeared at the window, very wet and white. 'Martha!' he said, slapping the glass with his hand. 'Martha! Shh! Quietly! Open the window.' He laughed. 'Quick, Martha, before I fall onto the wheelie bin!'

She opened the window and the rain came in and wet her face.

'What are you doing? You can't stay here or they'll catch you and put you in prison. There isn't a wheelie bin,' she added.

'Never mind that. Come with me now. Climb onto my shoulders, and put Tug under my arm and let's be off.' He was giggling.

'You're drunk,' she said.

'We'll be runaways!' he shouted. 'Shh!' he added. 'Quietly does it.'

She stared at him. It was too much. She felt herself begin to tremble. 'Stop it, Dad. Please stop. You're being silly.'

'What's wrong with being silly if we love each other? I love you more than . . . damn, I can't think of anything.' He began to laugh again. 'There's too much rain to think.' He took both hands off the ladder and reached them out towards her. 'Everything's my fault,' he said. 'Even the rain. I just wanted to see you. I miss you so much. Don't you miss me?'

Martha stepped backwards into her room. She was trembling so badly now she could hardly stand. Something was happening to her. She couldn't control herself any more. She felt a great shuddering

235

inside her, and a choking pain and her eyes were suddenly blind with tears.

'Leave me alone!' she screamed at the top of her voice.

Dad looked startled. 'Shh!' he said. 'Bit noisy.'

She ran forward and slammed the window shut. 'I don't want to see you any more!' she yelled.

Dad had stopped laughing. He pressed his face against the wet window pane, looking very surprised. 'Martha?' he mouthed.

She took a deep, deep breath, and shouted at him so furiously she hurt her throat: 'Can't you see? *I'm only a little girl!*'

Finally he was quiet.

Through the wet window he stared at her in horror. Then there were footsteps in the hall, and Grandma and Grandpa burst into the room, closely followed by Tug. From outside came a tilting, scraping, sliding noise. Then a thump and a muffled cry. Martha ran forward and looked down into the garden, just in time to see Dad, covered in mud, limping and slithering across the wet grass, round the side of the house and out of her life.

35

The seasons changed. Summer ended, autumn began. In the park the trees shed their leaves, the yellow and blue boats were taken off the lake and put into storage, and the tennis courts were locked up. At the end of October the café closed. The days grew short. Down by the canal where the fun fair used to come, work began on two new apartment blocks, and by the end of the year the walls were built up to the eaves. Christmas came and went, and then, very slowly, the dreary, colourless days of January and February, with their chilly mornings and gloomy afternoons, when Martha caught a cold and Tug had a verruca, and Grandpa developed bronchitis and had to stay in bed for nearly a week. In March the corner shop where they bought their lollies was replaced by a coffee shop, and road works went up all along the main road and kept the traffic at a crawl until the end of April.

During these months everything was strange and

new for Martha and Tug. As the seasons changed, they changed too. Martha stopped going to Cookery Club and Costumes Club; she took more interest in her school work and excelled, particularly in Science and Maths. She started playing hockey and did well enough to get into the school team, though the games teacher was apt to comment that she looked a little thin. She kept her long hair braided, and her friends at school told her she looked like Heidi or some other girl heroine in a foreign story. They all knew what had happened at home, and were sorry for her, and kind to her, though Martha never spoke about Dad to them. At the beginning of December she turned twelve, and Grandma and Grandpa took her for high tea at the Dorchester hotel in town. She was becoming a quiet, serious girl.

Tug, on the other hand, was neither quiet nor serious. He was growing fast. He wasn't neat and square any more, but dirty-faced and wiry, with big clumsy feet. He didn't like school. His behaviour in class had never been good; now he got into trouble regularly. His teachers reported that he was 'difficult and stubborn'. Once in the winter term, and twice in the spring term, Grandma and Grandpa were summoned to discuss his naughtiness with the head teacher. He had his sixth birthday in February, but Grandma and Grandpa didn't take him anywhere.

After that chaotic night at the end of August, Dad never came back. Grandma told the children that he had gone away to 'get better'. One autumn afternoon Martha and Tug secretly went to their old house to check, and saw another family living there, and knew then that Grandma was telling the truth. Martha asked Grandma where Dad had gone, but she said she didn't know. The number of Dad's phone had been cancelled, so they couldn't phone him, and Martha and Tug had new phones with new numbers, so he couldn't phone them. They received no messages or letters either, or even postcards. He had gone.

It was a relief. Almost immediately Martha began to feel better. She stopped getting the dizzy feeling. For a while she still got upset whenever she thought about Dad, but she made a conscious effort not to think about him, and as the months went by it got easier.

Her new life with Grandma and Grandpa was completely different, not at all confused, but very quiet and orderly. She didn't have to get breakfast for everyone, or find something to make for Tug's tea, or put herself to bed, or worry about what was going to happen. She didn't have to make lists any more. Everything was done for her. There were set times for getting up and having meals and going to bed, and scheduled activities to keep her and Tug busy, like visiting museums and going to Sunday school, and dozens of little things to remember such as looking at people when talking to them or closing doors quietly. At meal times they were encouraged to 'make conversation' about what they had just been doing. All their time was accounted for, even the minutes and seconds. It was highly organized. It was also, as Tug had said, tiring.

Curiously, though, Martha sometimes felt as if she wasn't properly busy. There were many things she was not allowed to do. Grandma didn't let her help with cooking ('It's a safety issue,') or look after Tug ('I shall monitor Christopher myself, thank you,') or sew in the house ('Grandpa and I can afford to buy you new clothes, should you need them.'). From the beginning Grandma made her views about children plain. She told them frequently – angrily – that Dad had given them far too much freedom.

'Children need rules,' she said. 'I warn you now, I will not make the same mistakes your father made.'

She could be strict, sometimes cold. Although she

encouraged 'discussion', she was not easy to talk to.

However, Martha soon discovered something Grandma would always talk to her about: Mum.

Living with Dad, Martha had got used to never talking about her. But in Grandma's house, there was no way of avoiding it. There were photographs of Mum everywhere – on the walls of the living room, on the sideboard in the dining room, along the bookcase in Grandpa's study, in the hallway, up the stairs, even in the downstairs toilet. Many of them showed Mum when she was a girl, with pale skin and red hair and a pointed nose.

'You're so alike,' Grandma said to Martha. 'I don't just mean the colouring, or the features. You have the look too.'

'What look, Grandma?'

Grandma smiled. 'Very determined.'

'Really?'

'Oh yes. You're a very determined girl, just as she was. I can tell.'

Grandma liked to talk to her about Mum when she was a girl, her ballet lessons, her struggles with homework, and, above all, her acting in school shows.

'She was always superb in whatever part she played. And she was always acting, whether or not she was on stage, putting on funny voices, dressing up, making up little songs.'

When Grandma talked about Mum like this she became a different person, warmer and kinder, easily distracted. At first it was strange. But Martha got used to it. She got used to the pictures too. Sometimes she went round the house, just looking at them. They made her feel sad, because Mum had died, but somehow they made her happy as well, as she imagined the sort of girl that Mum had been and thought about the stories Grandma told her.

It was not the same for Tug. He didn't talk to Grandma about Mum. He didn't talk to Grandma at all, if he could help it. But Grandma talked to him, mainly about the house rules and why he shouldn't have broken them.

'She's always telling me off,' he complained to Martha. 'Just because there's a bit of mud got onto the carpet, or the door bangs. If I ask her where the biscuit tin is she says I'm rude. I'm not rude, I'm *hungry*. And I didn't mean to drop my milk on that rug. And what's the point of Grandpa? *He* doesn't help.'

In fact, Grandma told Grandpa off too, for not saying the right thing, or for failing to be 'sufficiently firm' with the children, or for losing his glasses, which was often. Twice he had left them in Tug's room and it was hardly Tug's fault that both times he had trodden on them. But mainly it was Tug Grandma told off. She told him off for not speaking when he was spoken to, and for speaking when he shouldn't have been, and for not eating his salad, and for bringing earth into his room, and for cleverly inserting his third-best JCB into the pipe that fed the water-feature in the garden. At the appropriate times she told him off for his poor school reports. When he started to wet the bed again, she was cross with him about that too. And when at last, inevitably, he broke one of the Swarovski crystal figurines, she was very cross indeed.

'I hate flamingos,' Tug said. And this was true, because three weeks later, he broke another one.

Martha always defended Tug, though it didn't make much difference, and sometimes it seemed to make things worse.

As the months went by, Tug grew steadily unhappier.

'I'm going to run away.'

'No, you're not, Tug.'

'Yes, I am, Martha.'

'Where will you go?'

'I'll go back to Dad.'

243

'We don't know where Dad is.'

Unlike Martha, Tug talked about Dad a lot. He wanted to know where he was, and what he was doing, and why he never came to see them any more.

'Do you think he has a new family, Martha?'

'I don't know.'

'With a new Tug? And a new Martha?'

'I don't know, Tug.'

'But when will we find out?'

'I think, Tug, it might be better if we try to forget Dad, at least for a while. It only makes us sad.'

'Can you forget him?'

'I'm trying to. It's easier than you'd think. And it'll make you feel better.'

Tug said he would try too. 'But I still hate the flamingos,' he said. 'And Grandmas,' he added.

Every couple of months Martha and Tug had an interview with Alison from the Social Services. In these interviews they were asked lots of questions about living with Grandma and Grandpa, and – as Alison pointed out to Tug – their answers always showed that they were well looked-after, well-fed and safe.

36

If Grandma's weekly routines could seem dreary and tiring, at least Martha and Tug were still allowed to go to Marcus's every Wednesday.

One Saturday afternoon in September, shortly after they first moved in with Grandma and Grandpa, Marcus came to the house unannounced.

Grandma opened the door and found him on the doorstep wearing a tight-fitting catsuit made of gold lamé, and eye-liner.

'Good afternoon,' he said politely. 'You must be Martha's elegant grandmother. My name is Marcus Brown. May I speak to Martha?'

His good manners confused Grandma, who invited him in, even though Martha was out. She noticed that Marcus was carrying a bag. It was a plastic hand-bag printed with a leopard-skin design in pink.

'May I leave something with you, to give to her?'

Grandma said he may, and Marcus took out of the bag a long bright green piece of stretchy fabric.

'This is a mankini.'

'I beg your pardon.'

'An article of clothing for men. Quite sexual. It fits like this.'

Grandma watched, horrified, as he strapped it on over his catsuit.

'What do you think?' he asked Grandma. 'I think it's slightly vulgar.'

'I quite agree,' she said coldly.

'It's the green,' Marcus said. 'Exactly the wrong colour. And this fabric is all wrong too. I would like Martha to make me one in artificial fur.'

Grandma was bewildered. 'Artificial fur?' she repeated.

'Yes. Are you keen on artificial fur?'

'I am not.'

'You can get some quite nice stuff in electric blue. I've seen it.'

Grandma refused to take the mankini from Marcus and showed him out. That evening she talked to Martha about it, and put her view with characteristic plainness.

'I do not like the idea of you having anything to do with clothing to be worn by this boy. It is very far from proper. I must insist you cease to be involved.'

Martha was dismayed. 'But, Grandma, Wednesday nights are so much fun. Tug likes them too.'

'Obviously he will also have to stop going.'

'And Marcus needs our help.'

'Your only involvement is with the clothing, I think. I'm sure he will find someone else. I'm sorry, Martha. It's best to make a clean break and not see him any more.'

From Grandma's tone of voice it was clear that the 'discussion' was over, and she rose to go.

Martha thought fast. 'Grandma?'

'What is it?'

'If I can't make the costumes, I would like to act.'

As soon as she said it, she had the feeling that she had always meant to say it one day.

'Pardon?'

'I would like to act in Marcus's films. He's often asked me, and I've always said no. But I've changed my mind. Now I really want to.'

Grandma sat down again. She frowned. 'What films are these?'

'*My Fair Lady. Casablanca.*'

Grandma was surprised. 'They are good films, it's true,' she said.

'I want to do what Mum did,' Martha said.

The change came over Grandma. She smiled to

herself. 'Once, in fact, your mother acted in the school production of *My Fair Lady*. I remember it very well. There is a photo of her in Grandpa's study, I must show you.'

'She was such a very good actress, wasn't she, Grandma?'

Grandma nodded again. 'Though,' she added sternly, 'I'm not at all sure the acting world was good for her in the end.'

Martha said, 'This is just at a friend's house, so you needn't worry. I won't have anything to do with costumes any more, I promise. I'll just act.'

Grandma sighed. 'You're just like her,' she said. 'I suppose I shall have to let you have your way. So long as it doesn't get too serious.'

'It's just a bit of fun,' Martha said. She reached out and held Grandma's hand. 'Thank you.'

Grandma nodded.

'I'm going to try to be a good actress. Like Mum.'

And Grandma nodded again, and smiled, and fished in her bag for a handkerchief.

So after Martha's splint came off in October Grandpa drove her and Tug to Marcus's every Wednesday evening, where they worked together on their new speed films.

It was awkward the first time they went back, not least because Grandpa insisted on coming in and being introduced to Mr and Mrs Brown, who were, in turn, confused about what he wanted.

'Just checking that there are some responsible adults around,' he said, and Mr and Mrs Brown peered about them vaguely, as if hoping to find some.

It was awkward meeting Marcus and Laura again too. It was the first time Martha and Tug had seen them since just after the car crash six weeks earlier.

'What's it like,' Laura asked, 'living with your grandparents?'

'All right,' Martha said.

'Bloody horrible,' said Tug, who was trying out some of Laura's mannerisms.

'I met your grandmother,' Marcus said. 'She seemed like a nice old bird.'

Tug scowled. 'You wouldn't say that if she fed you salad.'

Laura asked, 'How's your father doing?'

'He's gone away for a little while.'

'Where to?'

'We don't know.'

There was a silence after this.

'I think it's for the best,' Martha added.

Marcus said in a normal voice very unlike his usual one, 'If ever you need anything, if ever you want to talk, if ever you just want company, I'm here, Laura's here. You know that, don't you?'

Martha nodded.

Then he cleared his throat and said, in his usual theatrical voice, 'But in the world of media celebrity we look forward, not back. A new challenge, a new dawn, a new working partnership. For the first time, Speed Version Productions will feature Martha Luna in the starring role. And I, Marcus Versace Brown, will create her wardrobe.'

37

Marcus told Tug the story of *Gone with the Wind*. 'It's very simple. Rhett loves Scarlett. Scarlett loves Ashley. Ashley loves Melanie. Do you follow?'

Tug nodded thoughtfully.

'Scarlett marries Charles, whom she doesn't love. Charles dies of measles. So Scarlett marries Frank. She doesn't love him either. Are you with me?'

'Yes.'

'Frank gets killed. So at last Scarlett marries Rhett. And he leaves her. Good, isn't it?'

Tug gazed at him. It was hard to tell what Tug was thinking.

'Did you listen to any of that?' Marcus asked.

'No,' said Tug, who had been thinking about biscuits. 'I was thinking about the songs.'

'There aren't any songs. There are a lot of deaths. Would you like to be killed?'

'I'd rather be second grip.'

'He's getting quite stubborn, isn't he?' Marcus said to Martha. 'Quite ferocious, aren't you, little Tug? All right, you can be second grip. Laura, watch out, he's a terrible man for the equipment. Martha, let me show you how the curtain dress should be worn.'

Now that Marcus was doing costumes he was more flamboyant and enthusiastic than ever. He had made two dresses for Martha. One was the 'garnet gown', which Scarlett wears to a party. It was red and flouncy with lace, feathers and tassels. The shoulders were so big Martha couldn't see sideways. The other was a calico dress which, in the film, Scarlett makes herself from curtains. So Marcus had made it from curtains, not his own curtains, of course, which were essential for keeping daylight out of the studio, but the curtains in his parents' room. The dress was a purple and lilac stripe with blackout lining and a valance, which didn't quite work, but which certainly looked like it was made from curtains. Both dresses were trimmed with electric-blue artificial fur and Marcus was very proud of them. 'The most beautiful of all my creations,' he called them, though in fact they were his only creations. He was sad not to be wearing them himself.

The first scene they filmed was the famous final

scene, when Rhett leaves Scarlett for ever. It was Martha's debut performance. They killed all the lights except for a single spot, and after a moment Martha stepped into it, wearing the curtain dress, and stood there very still.

They all stared at her in astonishment. It was as if she had become a different person.

Her face glowed, and slowly her eyes filled with tears. The tears spilled out and ran down her cheeks.

('Zoom in!' Marcus whispered in excitement to Laura. 'She's acting!')

'Rhett!' Martha cried, and her voice was different too, thrillingly clear and troubled. 'Rhett! Wait for me!'

She turned her head and gazed in distress at the far wall. 'Rhett! If you go, where shall I go, what shall I do?'

Slowly she sank to her knees, all the time her face glowing and her tears shining, saying in a low, tremulous voice, 'What is there to do, what is there to matter?' until she faded to silence.

No one said anything, or even moved.

Getting to her feet, Martha briskly wiped her face and said to Marcus, 'You forgot your line.'

Marcus found his voice at last. 'You don't need any

lines from me,' he said. He stood staring at her, almost humble with excitement. 'You're going to be a star.'

Tug sidled up, gazing at her timidly, and touched her, to check that she was still Martha.

Even Laura was impressed. 'Not bad at all,' she said.

Martha allowed herself a smile. She was pleased with herself. She had always wondered what it would feel like, finally, to act, and now it seemed to her that she had always known. It was only a question of self-control. Yet how strange that she could make herself cry, and actually feel sad, without thinking of anything. It was as if she wasn't only Martha, but other people too, and could become them very easily. It gave her a weird feeling.

Afterwards, she did most of the acting in Marcus's speed films. She was superb. She could make herself cry, do accents, sing, fall without hurting herself, pretend to die and a hundred other life-like things. Sometimes she seemed a little reserved, as if not quite emotionally engaged, but her technical skill always pulled her through. Above all, she had what Marcus called 'star quality', an expression, a sort of stillness, which made everyone want to look at her.

'How did you learn it all?' Laura asked.

Marcus answered for her. 'She didn't. It's a gift. It comes from her mother. I could tell. I spotted her. I shall make it all clear in my memoirs.'

So a new phase of speed films began. Like all Marcus's films, they were golden classics. When they finished *Gone with the Wind* in November, they filmed *The Blue Angel*, with Martha playing a nightclub singer called Lola Lola, wearing a (fur-lined) black-and-white cabaret costume with tassels and a top hat. That took them until Christmas. After that, they did *Notorious*, in which she was the daughter of a Nazi spy, wearing a classic black skirt suit and (fur-lined) 1940s mesh hat. Then *It's a Wonderful Life*, with Martha doubling as Mrs Bailey, dressed in a simple shirt-waist dress of cotton (and fur), and Clarence Odbody, Angel Second Class, appearing in an ankle-length white (fur-edged) nightdress.

Finally, at the beginning of April, they started work on *Brief Encounter*, in which Martha, playing a war-time suburban housewife, is parted for ever from her secret lover.

She was always marvellous, and as time went by even her costumes got better. She was happy. And at some point between the making of *Notorious* and *It's a Wonderful Life* she realized that she had succeeded in not remembering Dad. She hadn't forgotten him, but she rarely thought about him any more. It was as if she had finally said goodbye to him in her mind, and it was – as she had always known it would be – for the best.

38

After Easter the weather brightened. In the park the flowerbeds were full of pansies and marigolds, and fresh green leaves started to appear on the trees. The café re-opened, the boats were put back on the lake and the lawns were given their first mowing of the year.

Martha went through the park to fetch Tug from his school. Generally he was waiting for her at the school gates, though sometimes he was waiting in the head teacher's office.

Today, unfortunately for him, he was in the office. Martha went in and, after a short, one-sided conversation with the head teacher, collected Tug and also a letter to give to Grandma and Grandpa, and they went out together into the spring sunshine.

'What's the letter about, Tug?'

'Rudeness.'

'Who were you rude to?'

'Miss Savonarola.'

'Why?'

'I can't remember. But the letter will say.'

They crossed the road and went down the street, into the park. They went past the tennis courts and the café, and walked in a roundabout way across the grass to avoid the geese by the pond. They didn't talk. They were lost in their own thoughts. Martha was wondering how many times she had crossed the park in her life, and how many more times she would cross it. Every time she crossed it, she thought, she was a little bit different. And when she had crossed it enough times she would be grown up.

They went past the ornamental flowerbeds towards the park gates.

'Do you remember, Tug, that time when Grandma and Grandpa were waiting for us?'

'No.'

'Last summer. They bought us ice creams.'

'No.'

'And I kicked you under the table.'

Tug turned to her. 'Yes, you did. And it hurt.'

'Doesn't it seem like a long time ago now?'

'Will they be waiting for us today?' he asked uneasily.

'No.'

They turned the corner to the gates and Grandma and Grandpa were nowhere to be seen. A man was waiting there. A tall, thin man with a beard, wearing a smart grey suit.

At once Tug stopped and squeezed Martha's hand. 'What is it, Tug?'

Tug was staring at the man. 'Martha,' he said in a small voice.

'Don't be frightened, it's just a man in a suit.'

'But, Martha.'

The man with the beard came towards them, and Martha stared at him too, and the closer he came the more he looked like Dad.

'Don't be frightened,' Dad said. He stopped several paces away and stood there quietly. 'How are you?'

They were speechless.

'You don't have to talk to me,' Dad said. 'I just wanted to see you. It's been such a long time.' He smiled, and they could only just see the smile through the beard.

'You've grown,' he said.

'You've got a beard,' Tug said.

'Yes, I have.'

'It's an old beard.'

They all smiled at the grey hairs in Dad's beard.

The beard made him look different. It was hard to know what he was thinking as he stood there, looking at them.

'Now I have to go,' he said.

'Why?'

'Because I'm not allowed to see you. And because you don't trust me. Quite right too. But I'll see you again. Look for me by the park gates after school.'

'Dad?'

'Yes, Martha?'

He stopped and turned back to face her. It wasn't just the beard that made him look different. His eyes and nose looked different too. His voice sounded softer. And the way he stood, angular in his loose suit, and the way he looked at her, with a frowning, peering look – these things were different as well. In fact, there was nothing about him Martha recognized. And it was so shocking that for a moment she just stared at him.

'Yes?' he said again.

She saw him smile, hesitantly, through his beard.

'Where did you go?'

'Away. But just for a couple of months. Then I came back.'

'Where do you live now?'

'In our house, of course.'

'But there's another family living there.'

'Gone now. I rented the house to them until Christmas. After that, I moved back in.'

'So you've been there all this time, and we didn't know. Why didn't you tell us?'

Dad glanced at her sharply. 'Don't you get my letters?'

'What letters?'

He looked as if he was going to say something, then he didn't. 'Never mind,' he said.

He stepped forward and held their hands, and kissed them on the tops of their heads. His beard scraped their hair. Then he walked away.

'Look for me by the gates,' he called back, as he went.

During that evening's extended reading (seven thirty to eight thirty), Martha didn't read her library book. She didn't even open it. For the first time in months she was thinking about Dad again.

Now that he had reappeared her mind was filled with questions about him. She wanted to know if he had a new job, or a new family, what he spent his time doing, if he thought of them, what sort of person he was now. Above all, she wanted to know if he had stopped drinking.

She hadn't been able to tell anything about him from the way he looked in the park.

Although she wasn't supposed to, she left her room and tiptoed down the landing into Tug's.

'Tug?'

She switched on the light and Tug sat up, rubbing his eyes.

'You have to help me.'

'Help you how?'

'Do you remember what Dad said, about the letters?'

'He said he'd written us letters. But he hadn't.'

'I think he had.'

Tug finished rubbing his eyes and thought about it.

'I think Grandma's kept them from us,' she said.

'Why?'

'To stop us thinking about Dad.'

Tug thought about that.

'That's very naughty of her,' he said at last.

'Yes, it is.'

'Good,' he said with feeling. 'I'm glad. Usually it's me who's naughty,' he added.

'Where did she put them?' he asked after a while.

'I don't know. She might have thrown them away, I suppose. But perhaps she kept them somewhere.' Martha frowned. 'It's important, Tug. I think we should try to find them. They might tell us things about him, like if he has a new job.'

'Or a new family.'

'Yes.'

'All right.' Tug got out of bed. 'We're good at finding things, aren't we?'

'But not now, Tug. We have to wait until they go out.'

'But they never go out. Not without us.'

'Then we'll have to think of a plan.'

'What plan?'

'I don't know yet. You have to help me.'

39

Next day was Saturday. At 10.30 a.m., according to his schedule, Tug was supposed to be tidying his room. But he wasn't.

There was a sudden loud cry from somewhere outside.

Grandma, who was reading a letter at the kitchen table, got up and went to the window. 'Whatever is happening?' she said. She took off her reading glasses.

There was more noise: hoarse shouting and desperate yelling.

'Martha?' she called.

But Martha did not appear. Grandma tutted.

The noise grew louder. Oddly, it sounded now like singing – wild singing, badly out-of-tune. Grandma thought she detected the words 'bear' and 'mountain'. Collecting Grandpa from his study, she went out into the garden, and there they found Tug stuck at the top of the tallest fir tree, clinging to a slender branch overhanging the very breakable greenhouse.

When she was sure that Grandma and Grandpa were fully occupied, Martha crept out from the downstairs toilet and went quietly into Grandpa's study.

She didn't know if Dad's letters would be in the study, but she knew that Grandpa kept some box files on a high shelf, and she thought she would look there first. She climbed onto his desk to reach them. There were about ten files, all different colours, labelled *Bank*, *House*, *Car* and so on. But it was soon clear that none of them contained Dad's letters. Next she tried the desk drawers, where she found a box of pencils, a ball of rubber bands, a packet of paperclips, a pad of writing paper with matching envelopes and several back issues of the *Church Gazette*. Under the gazettes were some cigarette papers and a very creased copy of a newspaper called *The Racing Post*. There was nothing else. Finally she looked along the bookshelves. Propped against the books were a number of postcards, birthday cards and invitations, but although she examined them all carefully, none was from Dad.

She frowned. Her plan had failed.

Hearing Grandma and Grandpa coming back up the garden, she was just leaving when something on the top shelf caught her eye. She stopped still, and stared. It was a photograph of Mum when she was young, dressed in an old-fashioned gown. Something about it gave Martha a funny feeling, and she took the picture down and examined it. On the back someone had written *My Fair Lady, Christmas 1980*. Her heart began to beat fast. Mum had been twelve years old – the same age as Martha now. In the picture Mum was pale and smiling, her small nose pointed determinedly at the camera, and her hair was braided in two long plaits, just like Martha's. Martha stared. It was like looking at herself. And at the same time it was like being someone else. It gave her such a strange feeling. Though she felt like bursting into tears she could feel herself smiling as well.

But she had no time to think about it. She heard voices very near in the kitchen and, jamming the picture back on the shelf, she made a dash for the door.

'No, Christopher,' Grandma was saying, 'I don't understand why you threw your best JCB into the tree. Nor do I understand how it got wedged in a bird's nest. And I certainly don't know why you felt it necessary to "rescue" it yourself instead of informing us. Grandpa has a perfectly good ladder. Martha!' she called. 'There you are at last. Will you please help me make Christopher understand that our trees are not there to be climbed?'

It was some time before Martha and Tug could meet in private. But after Tug had spent an hour alone in his room, in order to reflect on Trees and What They Are There For, Martha was allowed to take him a glass of water.

He was sitting happily on his bed playing with his toes.

'I nearly fell into the greenhouse,' he said proudly. 'And Grandma was *very* cross.' He was thoughtful for a moment. 'I don't think she's ever been crosser,' he said with satisfaction. 'Did you get the letters?'

Martha confessed that she didn't. 'I'm sorry, Tug.'

'That's all right, Martha. I got one.'

He retrieved a very creased piece of paper from his underpants and handed it to her.

'What's this?'

'Grandma dropped it in the garden, and I found it.'

Martha looked at it. It was part of a letter.

'I found it,' Tug repeated. 'I didn't steal it. Is it from Dad?'

Incredibly, it was.

'She must have just got it this morning,' Martha said. 'I expect that's what she was reading at the kitchen table when you started to sing.'

'We're good at finding things, aren't we, Martha?' Tug said happily.

'There's only one page of it,' Martha said. 'It must have been longer. But it's definitely from Dad. Listen.'

She read the letter to Tug:

gets warmer it starts to itch. I worry that it makes me look old and simple, but then I am old and simple, so that's OK.

I had my last session with my Alcohol Counsellor today. I thought of the first time I went to see him, and how I couldn't bring myself to tell him the truth. Now I feel I could tell him anything. I've changed that much at least.

I've been swimming twice this week. Crikey, it's boring. And there's bloody water everywhere, as Laura once very truthfully said.

I've also tidied my room (again). And soon I hope to hear about my interview.

What are you doing, I wonder. I will try to guess. I think that you, Tug, have persuaded Grandma to build you a JCB scrambler track across her lawn. And you, Martha, have just

'Just what?' Tug asked.

'I don't know. That's where the page ends.'

They were silent for a while, listening to Dad's voice in their heads.

'Martha?'

'Yes?'

'What's a scrambler track?'

But Martha didn't tell him. She was thinking. 'I think he's written us lots of letters,' she said thoughtfully. 'I think he's written to us every week, telling us what he's doing, and asking us what we're doing. And Grandma's kept all the letters from us.'

'It was very, *very* naughty of her, wasn't it?' Tug said.

Martha was still thinking. 'I think something else too.'

'What?'

'I think he's stopped drinking.'

40

Every day after that they looked for Dad at the park gates on their way home from school. He wasn't always there, but when he was he would sit with them on a bench for a few minutes, or on the swings in the play area, and talk to them about what he was doing – all the things he had told them about in the letters they never received.

'Have you written every week, Dad?' Tug asked.

'Twice a week.'

The first thing he told them was that he had stopped drinking. 'Since that night last summer,' he said. 'That night the penny finally dropped.'

'And are you all right, Dad?' Martha asked.

He shook his head. 'No. It was right, what you said once. I don't like it on my own.'

They knew then that he didn't have another family.

Dad wanted to know what they had been doing, and Tug told him, very honestly, how many flamingos he had broken (three, so far), and listed, very carefully, all the reasons why he hated Grandma.

'You shouldn't blame her, Tug,' Dad said.

'Why?'

'You should blame me.'

Dad wanted to know what Martha had been doing too, and one afternoon she told him about acting in Marcus's speed films.

'Acting now?'

'Yes.'

He looked thoughtful. 'Which film are you doing at the moment?'

'*Brief Encounter.*'

'Show me.'

'What, here?'

He nodded.

'All right. Do you know the bit at the end of the film, when she nearly throws herself in front of the train?'

'Yes.'

'And you can hear her thoughts?'

'Yes.'

She walked away across the play area, past the climbing alphabet, the roundabout and the see-saw, and stopped and turned, and stood there for a moment. She gathered herself together until she looked different: taller, older and much sadder. She cocked her head on one side and stared at the ground vacantly, as if lost in thought, then slowly lifted her face towards Dad and stared at him. She stared so hard he felt the hairs stand up on the back of his neck. Suddenly she ran towards him, with a look of pure terror on her face as if she were about to throw herself on the ground in front of him, but stopped at the last second and stood there, swaying backwards and forwards, as if she were trying to balance on the edge of something and at any moment might fall. Gradually she became still. Her face was white and dazed, her eyes unfocused. In a voice quite unlike her own – agitated, posh and tender – she began to speak: 'I meant to do it, Frank. I really meant to do it. I stood there trembling right on the edge. But I couldn't. I wasn't brave enough. I should like to be able to say that it was the thought of you and the children that prevented me. But it wasn't. I had no thoughts at all. Only an overwhelming desire not to feel anything ever again. Not to be unhappy again. Then I turned and went back into the refreshment room.'

And Martha turned, slowly, sadly, but self-controlled, and walked away as far as the climbing frame.

'What do you think?' she asked.

Dad just looked at her. She had never seen him look so serious.

'Wasn't it very good?'

He said quietly, 'It's extraordinary. You've got it. Just like she had it. You're a natural.' He went over and hugged her.

'Do you like doing it?' he asked.

She shrugged. 'I suppose so.'

'Why?'

Martha had never thought about that before.

She frowned. 'It's odd. When I pretend to be someone else, it feels *right* somehow. As if that's who I'm really meant to be.'

Throughout April they continued to meet Dad in the park. But their meetings had to be secret. Dad still wasn't meant to see them.

'Why?'

'Well, Tug. There's a court order. Do you know what a court order is?'

'Yes. Grandpa didn't read it. It's a sort of prison.'

Dad explained about court orders. 'Anyway,' he said. 'You can't trust me yet. You don't know me.'

'When can we trust you?'

'I don't know. It takes time.'

'But when? Next week?'

'I think we'll all know when it happens.'

They kept their meetings short, so Grandma and Grandpa didn't become suspicious. One afternoon, in fact, Grandma and Grandpa unexpectedly came into the park and nearly discovered them, and Dad had to escape behind the café.

('Who was that man you were talking to?' Grandma asked. 'That man with a beard.'

'Just a stranger,' Martha said, and Grandma warned them against talking to strange men with beards.)

Bit by bit Dad told Martha and Tug more about himself. He had spent six months on an alcohol counselling course, he said, and several weeks working with the 'Children in Need' team at the Social Services. Now that he was coming to the end of his courses, he had applied for a renewal of his visiting rights. He was also trying to get a job. His life seemed quiet and small and stable.

Martha tried to imagine it. She wanted to believe he'd stopped drinking. She wanted him to be like he used to be, before the drink. But when she saw him in the playground, bearded and frowning in his baggy suit, when he looked at her in that new peering way, or spoke to her in his new soft voice, he still seemed to be a stranger. She wasn't sure he would ever truly be Dad again.

Tug's view was different. He was always asking Martha how soon they could leave Grandma and Grandpa's and go home, now that Dad was back.

'Don't think about that, Tug.'

'Why?'

'We don't know what Dad's like now. He might not be the same.'

'Because of the beard?'

'I wasn't thinking of that.'

'But he can shave it away.'

'Don't get cross, Tug. It's nothing to do with the beard.'

'Then *why can't he keep it?*'

These conversations often ended in tears.

Tug complained to Dad himself, but Dad was not sympathetic.

'You have to stay where you are, at least for the time being,' he said. 'And you have to do as Grandma and Grandpa tell you.'

But Tug wouldn't.

'Soon we'll be allowed to see each other properly and more often,' Dad said.

He explained that his application for visiting rights was already submitted, and a decision was due. 'I've had my interview with Alison,' he told them. 'And my Alcohol Counsellor has written a recommendation. Now they just need to consult Grandma and Grandpa. So long as they agree, soon we can see each other every day, and you can come and stay at home with me several nights a week.'

But Tug wanted to stay straightaway.

'Good things come to those who wait,' Dad said. 'You just have to be patient.'

But Tug could not be patient. Over the next few weeks he was naughtier than ever at school, and at Grandma and Grandpa's he was openly rebellious. Even Martha told him off. He refused to eat his salad, and watched television after tea, and complained ceaselessly that he was hungry, and helped himself to biscuits from the biscuit tin. He broke a fourth flamingo. When Grandma talked to him, he answered back. And if she sent him to his room to consider Behaviour and How to Improve it, he escaped and went into the garden and climbed trees. He cried and shouted, and spilled more milk on the rug, and every night he wet the bed.

And at last he ran away.

41

It was a Saturday night in the middle of May. Just before going to bed, Grandma found the sole remaining Swarovski flamingo lying on the dining room floor. It wasn't the whole flamingo. Just the head. It looked up at her from the carpet with a snooty expression.

Carrying the head on the palm of her hand like a relic, she went upstairs in a fury, and into Tug's room.

'Young man,' she said. 'I would like to know the meaning of this.'

She switched on the light and saw then that the bed was empty.

'Christopher!' she called sharply. 'Come out from there.'

There was silence.

'Christopher?' she said.

At that moment she saw the note pinned to the pillow with something else she recognized with horror: a pair of slender rose-pink legs.

'Christopher!' she said a third time, very loudly.

Grandpa came hurrying into the room, wearing his dressing gown inside out, and when he had removed his glasses from his dressing-gown sleeve they read the note together. It was not a long note. It said:

It cam of in my hand. I hate you Flum Mingo. I hate you. You wont see me agen. I haf run a way.

   TUG (is my name)

Grandma lifted her head and called for Martha.

They searched in Tug's room and found nothing except for the middle bit of the Flum Mingo in his waste-paper basket. Then they searched the rest of the house, and after that the garden, though this was difficult because it was dark. Grandma's fury rapidly turned to anxiety.

'He has left the premises,' she said. 'What time is it?'

Grandpa informed her that it was eleven o'clock.

For the twentieth time she asked Martha if she knew anything at all about any of this, and looked at her disbelievingly when Martha said she didn't.

'Obviously he has taken himself off,' she said with a panicky gesture towards the road.

'Please,' Martha said. 'Can we phone the police now?'

They hurried inside, and as they reached the dining room the phone in Grandpa's study began to ring.

Grandpa answered it. 'Hello. Ah. When? Yes, right away. One thing before you go. I'm bound to be asked if you had anything to do with any of this. I see. Two minutes.' He put the phone down.

'He's at his father's house,' he said. 'He arrived there just now with nothing but a rucksack full of biscuits.'

'I didn't think Christopher could have organized this on his own,' Grandma said.

'His father says he had nothing to do with it.'

'His father says!' Grandma looked at Martha. 'Please go and put your clothes on.' She turned her gaze on Grandpa. 'Get the car out,' she said shortly.

At first Martha didn't recognize their old house. It had been painted. The hawthorn tree was neatly pruned and the wheelie bin was housed in a smart wooden shelter. When Dad let them in, she saw that the inside of the house had changed too. The old carpets had been taken up, and the floorboards sanded and polished. They glowed with a golden waxy glow. The walls were freshly painted: buttermilk in the hallway, sage green in the front room and cornflower blue in the kitchen. The kitchen had completely changed: there were new terracotta tiles on the floor, and blue-and-white ornamental tiles on the walls above the work surfaces, and new pine cabinets which matched the new pine table. Outside, at the back, the patio was lit up, and through the window Martha could see that it had been rebuilt with pretty sandstone flags. Standing on it was a set of smart wrought-iron furniture painted green.

She didn't recognize Dad at first either: he had shaved off his beard and he looked much younger: lean-faced and sombre.

Tug was sitting at the new kitchen table. There was pie round his mouth. When he saw Grandma and Grandpa, he got up and came across to them and said gruffly, 'I'm sorry, Grandma, for running away. It was wrong of me.' He gave Grandma a box, and looked at Dad, and Dad nodded at him. Then they all went into the front room and Dad brought out a pot of coffee.

Grandma still looked cross, though Martha could tell that the newly-decorated house had impressed her.

She put on her glasses and opened the box. Inside was a Swarovski flamingo.

'Well,' she said, and it was impossible to tell what she meant.

Dad said, 'I bought it some time ago. I had a feeling one might get broken. Now it seems we owe you another.'

'Well,' Grandma said, more quietly this time.

Dad began to talk to Grandma and Grandpa, and after a moment Martha asked to be excused and went upstairs with Tug.

'I want to check something,' she whispered to him. 'What thing?'

They went into Martha's room, and, as she had guessed, it was newly decorated and furnished. There was a high bed above a neat little desk, and a new wardrobe with a big mirror and a sign above it saying *Here's Looking at You, Kid*. On the desk were some new maths puzzles of the sort Martha liked, and some other games. There were new books on the book-shelves too, and on the wall several large framed black and white photographs of film actresses: Audrey Hepburn playing Eliza Doolittle in *My Fair Lady* and Ingrid Bergman as Ilsa in *Casablanca*, and various others. One of them Martha didn't recognize at first. She was a strikingly pretty woman wearing tennis whites and holding a racket, and after a moment Martha realized that it was Mum in her role in the television soap opera.

'Come and look, Martha!' Tug called excitedly, and she went down the hall to him. His room had been decorated too. The walls were JCB-yellow, and the new carpet was handily earth-coloured. There was a big string bag full of toys in the corner and a pile of books about How to Do Things, and a model kit of a jet aeroplane.

Tug grinned crazily as Martha looked round.

'But where's the bed?' she asked.

'I knew you wouldn't find it,' he said happily. 'I found it.' And he pulled a handle in the JCB-yellow wall, and the bed folded out smoothly into the middle of the room.

They heard Dad calling, and reluctantly went downstairs.

He was still talking to Grandma and Grandpa. The conversation was awkward – about court orders, among other things – but Martha noticed how calm Dad was. He was friendly to Grandma and Grandpa, and said how much he appreciated them looking after Martha and Tug.

'Knowing they're safe has made everything else possible,' he said. 'And I'm very grateful.'

He told them, in a quiet manner, about his alcohol counselling course, and the sessions with the 'Children in Need' team, and he explained that he had re-applied for visiting rights. 'Obviously, you'll be consulted,' he said.

Grandpa sighed. 'As far as I'm concerned,' he said, 'you're welcome to them. You've changed, I can tell. Besides,' he added, 'I've never been so tired in all my life as I have been this last year.'

Grandma gave Grandpa a sour look. 'I'm pleased to hear of your progress with your treatment,' she said to Dad. 'But now,' she added briskly, 'we really must go. Come along, Christopher.'

Tug frowned and looked at Dad.

'Off you go,' Dad said. 'I'll see you soon.'

'Can't I stay here with you?'

'Not yet.'

'When?'

'As soon as I'm allowed. Your room's ready for you. Did you see?'

Tug nodded.

'But for now you have to go back with Grandma and Grandpa. And I want you to promise me something.'

'What thing?'

'That you'll be good.'

Tug looked shifty.

'Tug!'

'All right.'

Dad saw them all out.

'Oh, I nearly forgot,' he said at the door. 'I've got a new job.'

'Is it with pets?' Martha asked anxiously.

'No. The poodles of the world can breathe easy. I'm going to be a cinematographer again. Different television company. Same sort of job.'

'With cameras?' Tug asked.

'With cameras.'

'And a canteen?'

'With a canteen too.'

They all wished him luck.

'And Marcus will be pleased,' Martha said.

Grandma turned to her. 'Marcus Brown? Marcus Brown is a very strange boy.'

'I used to think that,' Dad said. 'But it's odd. The better you get to know him the more normal he seems.'

42

Spring turned to summer. June began with a blaze of sunshine. Old men in cardigans came out to sail their model boats on the pond in the park, and the rowing club took over the lake again. Joggers went round and round, and the tennis courts were full all afternoon and evening. People walked their dogs, and pushed pushchairs, and wheeled bikes, and some even sunbathed on the lawns.

While they waited for Dad's visiting rights to be granted their lives were the same as before at Grandma and Grandpa's. At first Tug was good, as he had promised, but as the weeks went by he found it harder, and by the middle of June he was tired and fretful. Although he hadn't broken any more Swarovski figurines, it was noticeable that Grandma was stricter with him since he'd run away. His daily tasks were closely monitored, and any misdemeanour, no matter how trivial, was followed by an interview with Grandma and a period alone in his room in order for him to focus his mind on Manners and How to Mind Them, Biscuits and Why it is Wrong to Steal Them, and Spit and Why it Should be Kept in the Mouth.

'But *when* will Dad's visiting rights be ready?' he kept asking Martha.

Eventually she began to feel fretful too. It was taking a long time for Dad to sort out his visiting rights. And she still felt unsure about him. He puzzled her. In many ways she still thought of him as a stranger, a man with unfamiliar mannerisms, who peered at her as if trying to read her mind, and left a pause before answering a question, and spoke slowly, sometimes hesitantly, and did a dozen other things that Dad had never done before. Despite her uncertainty, however, she was beginning to like him. He didn't look like the sort of man who would start drinking again. He was thoughtful too. He had bought a Swarovski flamingo for Grandma and decorated the house for them to come back to. The photograph of Mum playing tennis in her new room made her think of Dad teaching her to play when she was little, the safe feel of his arm round her and the warm rasp of his cheek against hers, and the smell of pear drops. As the days passed, she began to feel friendlier towards him, and at last, even though she didn't know him any better, she told herself that she would trust him.

To stop herself being fretful while she waited, she decided to take her acting more seriously. She got help at school. With her Drama teacher she learned about body language, with her Music teacher she trained her voice, and with her PE teacher she practised her movement. In the school library she found some books about acting techniques, and studied them in breaks and at lunchtime. She learned new things, like how to stand and how to be silent, how to follow the frame of the camera, how to breathe properly and control the volume and tone of her voice, and how to show emotion: to suffer pain, and laugh with joy, and have a fit, and be in love. On Wednesday evenings she discussed camerawork and lighting with Laura, and costumes and make-up with Marcus, and together they worked out different ways of playing her scenes in *Brief Encounter*. The harder she worked at her acting, the more she liked it. When she stood in front of the camera – as Alec Harvey (mackintosh collar turned up, hat brim turned down) or Laura Jesson (with demurely-waved hair and tightly-buttoned wool jacket) or Myrtle Bagot (sporting floral blouse and over-bright lipstick) – she felt most truly herself, and forgot to be fretful.

But a strange thing happened. Marcus became fretful instead. It was very unlike him. When they finished *Brief Encounter* – the longest and best film they had ever made – he couldn't decide what they should do next.

'I can't explain it,' he said, 'but I feel as if we should be doing *more*. Speed films were all very well when we were young. But look at us now. Outstanding first and second grips, one of Europe's leading costume designers' – turning to modestly acknowledge his reflection in the mirror on the back of the door – 'and, of course, the Greatest Movie Star of her Generation. But we can't afford to delay. I'm twelve already.'

It was vital, he said, to move to the next level.

'Keep your hair on,' Laura said. 'Just tell us what it is.'

'I don't know!' he cried, and went to stand in front of the mirror, making strange faces at himself.

'Bloody good job he's only Costumes,' Laura said.

But as the days went by, and they still couldn't decide what to do next, they all found it hard not to be fretful.

43

Then one day Dad was waiting for them again at the gates.

It had been over a month since they had seen him. They went into the playground and sat together on the swings.

He looked nervous. 'I shouldn't be here,' he said. 'Visiting rights haven't been granted yet, and I'm still not meant to see you.'

Martha and Tug groaned.

'I don't know what's holding them up. But I've got something else to tell you. About something that's happening at work.'

He told them that a film of *Anne of Green Gables* was being made. 'Do you know the book? It's about a little orphan girl in Canada. It's a classic.'

Martha had read it. 'I liked it,' she said. 'It's funny, but it's also sad.'

There had been films of it before, Dad said, but they were doing a new one, with a lot of Hollywood money behind it. 'It's going to be a big deal.' He paused. 'I thought of you, Martha.'

Martha was pleased. 'I'd like to see it. Can we go and see it together? When you get your visiting rights, of course.'

'I mean, I wondered if you wanted to be in it.'

Martha looked at him blankly. 'In it?'

'As Anne. They're auditioning for the part now.'

'Audition? *Me?*'

'Why not? It's just right for you. Anne's a girl about your age, with red hair and pale skin.'

'I'm not Canadian.'

'You can do accents.'

'But, Dad, you said it's a Hollywood film. I can't go over to Hollywood to audition.'

'They're having difficulty filling the part. Auditions are being held in lots of different places.'

'Like where?'

'Like in our studio here.'

There was silence.

Tug said, 'When you get the part, can I come with you to Hollywood?' He frowned. 'Will Grandma and Grandpa have to come too?'

Martha took hold of Dad's hand, and smiled. 'Thank you for thinking of me,' she said. 'But I don't think I can do it. You have to be really special to act in a Hollywood film.'

Without smiling, Dad took her other hand as well, and looked at her steadily. 'And I wouldn't ask you if I didn't think you were special.'

There was another silence.

'There's only one other person I've seen who was as good as you, and you know who that was. Besides, it's exactly the sort of old-fashioned thing you've been doing with Marcus. Honestly, you'd be perfect.'

Martha thought about it. 'Can anyone audition then?'

Dad looked shifty all of a sudden. 'Actually, it's by invitation only. You have to submit a DVD portfolio first. But,' he added quickly, 'you have lots of good stuff on film.'

'I don't know whether I want to send it in, though.'

Dad looked even shiftier. 'I already did.'

'*What?*'

'I got it from Marcus. He didn't know what it was for, so don't blame him.'

'Dad!'

'They liked what they saw. They've invited you to audition.'

Martha stared at him. Now she understood. She

stood there, not knowing what to say. What unexpectedly came into her mind was the photograph of Mum in Grandpa's study, dressed up for *My Fair Lady*, with her hair braided, smiling at her – and for an instant she dared to smile herself.

'Think about it anyway,' Dad said. He told her the date and time of the audition, and what she would have to do, and who the director of the film was (he had met him once in California), and lots of other details she was too excited to take in.

'If you decide to do it, you'll have to tell Grandma and Grandpa,' he said. 'They'll need to fill in forms for you, and take you to the studio, and so on. Although,' he added, wistfully, 'I could help, if they want me to. But best not to mention me at first. As I say, I'm not meant to see you.'

He looked at his watch. 'Look for me at the gates the day after tomorrow, and tell me what you're going to do.'

Then he went.

44

It was ridiculous to think about auditioning for a Hollywood film. But all the next day she couldn't stop thinking about it.

In the school library she found a copy of *Anne of Green Gables*, and as she read it she kept imagining what it would be like to play the part. She could hear Anne's voice in her head and see herself acting the scenes.

At lunchtime she went to find Marcus, who spent all his breaks nowadays in the Art room experimenting with fabrics, and there, among the tubes of paint and unidentifiable papier-mâché sculptures and half-finished self-portraits, she asked him what he thought – and he was so excited he nearly cross-stitched his thumb to a pair of lilac suede pants he was making.

'You think it's a good idea?'

'Not just a good idea. It's the next level! Martha, you're a genius, you've solved all our problems. I'll draw up a rehearsal schedule immediately.'

She frowned. 'You'd better wait a bit. I haven't made up my mind yet.'

'Yes, yes,' he said. 'And, of course, there'll be the audition costume to make. And what about your own brochure?'

'Marcus!'

He promised to wait.

That evening, after finishing her homework, Martha sat in her room reading *Anne of Green Gables*, and, without meaning to, often found herself acting out bits in front of the mirror. But every time she thought of auditioning she felt hot and breathless. She wished there was someone else she could talk to before deciding. Tug was too small.

Putting the book down, she wandered through the house with the same thoughts going round in her head. Did she dare audition? Did she dare do something just because she wanted to?

In every room there were photographs of Mum. Mum in her hockey kit. Mum in her school uniform. Mum standing on the stage dressed up for a show. Mum sitting in a chair. She had seen them all many times before, but now she found herself stopping to look at them again. If Mum were alive, what advice would she give her now?

Studying the pictures, she noticed that Mum nearly always had the same expression on her face. It was a curious expression, not just determined, as Grandma had said. She looked more closely. It looked as if Mum was smiling for the camera at the same time as thinking about something completely different. As if she had a secret. As if she knew something wonderful and important which she would tell you if only you asked.

Martha stared at the pictures. *What was it?*

She would never know.

But it was at that moment that she decided to go for the audition.

When she went upstairs to Tug's room and told him, he began at once to empty out all his drawers and boxes, and pile everything onto his bed.

'What are you doing?'

'Packing,' he said.

Martha explained about auditions, and helped him put everything back where it belonged. Then she went downstairs to find Grandma.

She had a fluttery feeling in her stomach. Although she didn't know what would happen at the audition – she didn't imagine she would get the part – she did allow herself to feel that perhaps her life was changing. Even more fluttery was the strange notion that she could try to *make* it change.

'No,' Grandma said. 'You may not.'

She sat upright at the kitchen table and spoke firmly.

Martha began again to talk about the audition, but Grandma interrupted her.

'It's out of the question.'

'But why, Grandma?'

'You're far too young. I don't approve of child actors in professional films.'

'Mum acted when she was a child.'

'Never professionally. I did not allow it.'

'Later she did.'

'Much later. As I've said before, I don't believe the film and television world was good for her. It is full of untrustworthy people.'

Martha began to talk about Mum again, but Grandma didn't soften as she usually did. She remained stern and disapproving.

'My mind is made up. I have let you act in the films of that boy so long as it did not become too serious. But now I must be firm.'

Martha couldn't think what to say to persuade her.

Instead she said, in a quiet voice, 'I really want to do it.'

Grandma said nothing, and Martha knew then that it was no good. Grandma would never allow her to go to the audition. She bit her lip. 'It's not fair.'

'It's not a question of what is and isn't fair, Martha. It's a question of what is for the best.'

'It is for the best. For me.'

Grandma pursed her lips. 'We must not always be thinking of ourselves. I know what a determined girl you are, Martha, and I realize how disappointed you are. But, really, there's no more to say.'

She took off her glasses and looked at Martha hard. 'How did you find out about this film?'

Martha remembered what Dad had said and hesitated. 'At school,' she said.

Grandma continued to look at her.

'There's a poster in the library.'

'I'm sorry, Martha,' Grandma said at last. 'But the answer is definitely no. Please don't risk upsetting yourself by asking me again.'

There was nothing else to say, and Martha went back up to her room.

When Tug came in, hours later, she was still sitting on her bed staring sadly at the wall. He climbed up beside her and put his head against her shoulder, and they stayed like that for a long time, in silence. At last, without saying anything, he gave her a biscuit, warm from being held so long and slightly broken, which he had stolen specially from Grandma, and went back to his own room.

45

The next day they met Dad in the park, and Martha told him what had happened. They walked together round the edge of the boating lake.

'What did she say?'

'That I was too young.'

She didn't tell him what Grandma had said about meeting untrustworthy people in film and television.

They walked round the lake again.

'Do you think she might change her mind?'

Martha shook her head. 'No. Never.'

They walked round the lake a third time.

Martha kept looking at Dad. She was upset enough herself, she didn't want him to be upset as well; she didn't think she could bear it if his face went pale and shiny, if he started to jerk his arms around or run his hands through his hair.

But he didn't do any of these things.

He smiled instead. 'Never mind. If Grandma won't help you, I will.'

It took her by surprise. 'But, Dad, you're not allowed. What about your court order?'

He put his finger against her lips. 'Don't worry about me. You've done enough worrying about me to last a lifetime. Worry about your audition, if you like.'

'But, Dad.'

'We'll do it together. In secret. No one will ever know. I can tell how much you want to do it. And I want to help you. The only question is: are you going to let me?'

Martha still hesitated.

'Put it this way,' he said. 'Do you trust me?'

And she nodded.

In any case, it was too late to stop Marcus. He had broken his promise. By the time Martha went back to his house, he had read the text, blocked out a selection of scenes for treatment and drawn up the rehearsal schedule. Martha's audition costume was already at the design stage, he said, and 'shaping up nicely'.

'Audition costume?'

'Leave it to me,' he said. '"Very short, very tight,

300

very ugly dress of yellowish-grey wincey." I quote from the book.'

'Wincey?'

'Like pyjamas. My only worry is that it won't exactly knock your eye out. I was wondering . . .'

'No fur, Marcus.'

'How strange,' he mused, 'that I should be making something deliberately ugly when my whole life has been dedicated to beauty.'

At the first rehearsal he told Tug the story of *Anne of Green Gables*.

'An old woman and her brother, farming in the wilds of Canada, decide to adopt a boy from an orphanage to help them on the farm.'

Tug thought that sounded reasonable.

'But there's a mistake, and they're sent a girl instead. She's quite mad, has an over-active imagination, a heart of gold and absolutely no common sense.'

Tug thought that sounded normal.

'She has a lot of misadventures. Gets her best friend drunk, dyes her hair green, accidentally poisons people. That sort of thing. Gilbert Blythe falls in love with her, so she smashes him over the head with a stone.'

Tug and Marcus thought about this together. 'It's a classic, apparently,' Marcus said. He looked disappointed. 'Between you and me, don't you think it sounds a bit too straightforward?'

Tug thought. 'Is there any food in it?' he asked.

'Now you mention it, I believe there's a pie.'

Tug said he thought it was a masterpiece.

The format of the audition was simple. Martha would present one scene of her own choice, and do one given to her by the director. For rehearsal purposes, they chose three scenes representing three different aspects of Anne – Angry Anne, Honest Anne and Imaginative Anne. Over the next three weeks, Martha practised them all.

Tug helped her learn her lines.

Laura filmed the scenes from different angles and under different sorts of lighting so Martha could study the shoots and make adjustments.

And Marcus ran everything. He also made the ugly dress, which, to everyone's relief, proved to be ugly in a very straightforward way.

Sometimes Dad came to Marcus's house. He talked to Marcus about general arrangements, and to Laura about technical issues. One afternoon he watched Martha rehearse.

'Imaginative Anne,' Marcus whispered to him. 'The first time she's done it.'

Martha appeared in the spotlight, lightly poised, her head cocked on one side. She was wearing Marcus's ugly dress, which made her look younger and needier and somehow more hopeful all at the same time. There was a twinkle in her eye. 'Now,' she said, peering about. 'I'm going to imagine things into this room so that they'll always stay imagined.' Her voice was bright and gleeful. 'The floor,' she said, squinting at Marcus's equipment-strewn carpet, 'is covered with white velvet rugs with pink roses all over them. And the walls,' she added, switching her attention to a dull stretch of wallpaper, 'are hung with gold and silver brocade tapestry.' Suddenly she straightened up. 'I can see my reflection in that splen-did big mirror,' she said, assuming a lofty expression. 'I am tall and regal, clad in a gown of trailing white lace, and my name,' she added – her mouth twitching briefly with fun – 'is the Lady Cordelia Fitzgerald!'

They all decided that she should perform Imaginative Anne as her chosen piece.

Her Honest Anne was equally good. But she had more difficulty with Angry Anne.

'I hate you!' she shouted, stamping her foot. 'I hate

you! I hate you! How dare you call me skinny and ugly? How dare you say I'm freckled and red-headed?'

There was no problem with her expression or movement, but her voice was slightly unconvincing. There wasn't enough emotion in it.

'Sometimes it's hard to make yourself really angry,' she said.

'Think of Grandma,' Tug said.

With Laura and Marcus's assistance, Martha worked hard on the scene, and it improved.

'Anyway,' Marcus said. 'You might not get an angry scene to do.'

For two weeks they practised everything, and on the day before the audition, Marcus addressed them all from in front of the mirror.

'Tomorrow our leading lady, Martha Luna, makes history with the first professional audition of her career. A moment for all our memoirs. Martha, would you like to say a few words?'

Martha wouldn't. She was beginning to feel nervous.

Marcus, who had no notion of what nerves were, went on smoothly. 'Then it only remains for me to thank you all for your hard work. Please be here tomorrow at nine o'clock sharp. We set off at quarter past. Mr Luna is our chauffeur. That's it. Take another look at the dress on your way out. Get a good night's sleep. Pray to your gods. And darling,' he said to Martha, 'prepare to conquer the world.'

46

On Saturdays Martha and Tug usually tidied their rooms and changed their bedding, and helped round the house. Today Martha had persuaded Grandma to let them go to Marcus's instead, to 'finish a new speed film'.

It hadn't been easy. Martha didn't like lying, and Grandma was suspicious.

'This is very inconvenient, Martha. Can't it wait till Wednesday?'

'All the costumes have to be returned to the shop by the end of Saturday.'

'What costumes?'

'A tea gown. And a petticoat.'

'What is the film?'

Martha hesitated. 'My *Fair Lady*.'

'I thought you'd done that one.'

'We're remaking it. It's a remake of the remake.'

Grandma frowned. 'Just this once then. Grandpa will take you. And pick you up no later than five o'clock. You'll have to tidy your rooms after tea.'

Sitting silently in the back of Grandpa's car at a quarter to nine on Saturday morning, Tug didn't dare look at Martha. She had explained to him very carefully that he mustn't say anything about the audition in front of Grandpa, and he sat next to her on the back seat staring the other way with both hands over his mouth.

'He hasn't got toothache, has he?' Grandpa asked.

'No,' Martha said. 'He's just got nothing to say.'

She had nothing to say either. Now that she was on her way to the audition, she felt more nervous about it than ever. She was also nervous about Dad. At the back of her mind was the fear that Grandpa or, even worse, Grandma, would find out he was violating his court order by helping them. He was due to pick them up at Marcus's just after Grandpa had left.

To Martha's dismay, when they got to Marcus's Grandpa insisted on coming into the house – as he occasionally did – to say hello to Marcus's mum and dad. He didn't seem to be in a rush to get back to Grandma.

'I think I might stay and watch a bit,' he said.

She began to panic. For a moment she thought that everything was going to go wrong before it had even started. But Marcus rescued the situation.

'Alas,' he said to Grandpa, 'we operate a sealed studio policy. No unauthorized personnel allowed during filming. It's the insurance,' he added, a phrase he often used in awkward situations. Adults were very sensitive to matters of insurance, he had noticed.

Grandpa left, not a moment too soon. Almost immediately afterwards, Dad arrived.

'And now,' Marcus said. 'Our date with glory.'

Gathering together their copies of the various scripts and Martha's costume, they got into Dad's car and set off, leaving Mr and Mrs Brown smiling vaguely at the door.

'They do not know,' Marcus said wistfully, looking back at them, 'that history is being made.' He checked his watch and smiled. They were exactly on schedule.

It was an hour's drive to the studios. Their excitement mounted steadily, and by the time they turned off the ring road and began the last stretch of the journey, the car was a hubbub of voices. Dad was explaining to Marcus how television companies organize their costume requirements, and Tug was asking Dad how television companies organize their canteens, and Marcus was telling Laura how celebrities organize their fame, and Laura was asking Dad what cameras professionals used. Everyone kept looking out for the first sight of the studios, and thinking they had seen them when they hadn't, and laughing at themselves.

Only Martha was quiet.

There was a up-and-down feeling in her stomach, and a gulp in her throat she couldn't quite swallow away. She tried to think of nothing, but it didn't work. Instead she found herself thinking about Mum, the way she looked in all those photographs, with that strange expression, as if she knew something wonderful and was about to tell her what it was, and never would. She wished Mum was with her now. With all the auditions she had been to, Mum must have known everything about up-and-down stomachs and ungulpable gulps; she would have known exactly what to recommend.

They parked in the studio car park and got out, everyone still talking and laughing.

Martha said in a small voice, 'Dad?'

'Yes?'

'I feel anxious.'

He gave her his hand, and she held it tightly.

'Are you going to stay with me?'

'Don't worry. Whenever you need me, I'll be here.'

They went into a building, through the security systems and down several corridors to the performers' room, where the other auditionees and their families were already waiting. They were quieter now, talking in whispers, but just as excited. From the auditions manager, they learned that it was the last round of auditions before the director flew home. There were fourteen candidates altogether, most from theatrical agencies, some from abroad. The most exciting news of all was that there were still no front-runners for the part.

Dad gave Martha's hand a squeeze. 'They really could choose someone here today,' he said.

According to the schedule they were given, Martha was last on the list. Dad read out the order of events.

'You need to have your hair done in three quarters of an hour. Then you go into make-up. Then wardrobe. Finally the audition room. That's at twelve fifteen. Excited?'

'I think so.'

'Nervous?'

She nodded. She still had hold of his hand.

310

They sat together in a corner of the room.

'Mum used to get nervous before auditions.'

'Did she know any trick to stop being nervous?'

'She did actually.'

'What was it?'

'Bananas.'

'Bananas? Did it work?'

'No. She never remembered to eat them.'

For a while they sat together in silence.

'Mum would be very proud of you,' Dad said quietly. 'And I'm very proud of you too. I'll be proud of you whatever happens in the audition. You won't forget that, will you?'

She shook her head, and gradually she began to feel better. Though she remained nervous, she was determined to do her best. She sat up straight and pointed her nose at the clock, and said to herself: *I don't need bananas because Dad's with me, and I don't mind if I don't get the part because Mum would be proud of me anyway, and if I do get the part even Grandma will have to be proud of me.*

At exactly the same time as Martha was thinking this, Grandpa's car was pulling up again outside Marcus's house. He had left his glasses behind.

He knocked at the door and waited.

When Mrs Brown opened it she stared at him in surprise.

'You've missed them,' she said, 'They've gone already. He came for them just after you left.'

It was Grandpa's turn to look bewildered. 'He?'

'Mr Luna.'

'Mr Luna?'

'To take them to the audition. History is being made,' she added proudly.

Grandpa's face fell into an unusual shape.

Twenty minutes later, when he got back home (rather breathless), it was Grandma's turn to be bewildered. Her bewilderment was brief, however. It was immediately replaced by righteous anger.

'I was right to be suspicious. Saturday morning rehearsals indeed. He has abducted them. Get me the number of the Social Services. Also his probation officer. And get the car out,' she called after Grandpa as he hurried from the room. 'We set off at once.'

It was a long wait in the performers' room, but Dad got them all drinks from the vending machine, and Laura had lots of good solid advice ('Relax, it's only bloody Hollywood,') and Tug drew an interesting picture of what he thought the canteen would look like, and Marcus kept them entertained with a long soliloquy about the Golden Age of Hollywood Costumiers.

At last Martha's name was called.

'This is it,' Dad said.

They crowded round her one last time, wishing her luck, then she took her ugly dress and her other things, and walked away from them, out of the room.

Dad sighed and looked at his watch. 'Well,' he said. 'Now we wait a bit more. Any questions?'

Tug wanted to know where the canteen was.

'Later, Tug.'

'Isn't it lunch time?'

'We have to have a late lunch today. It's OK, the canteen stays open. Any other questions?'

Marcus wanted to know if they could watch the audition.

The auditions manager said it wasn't allowed, but Dad had an idea. 'If we go into the director's box for the studio next to the audition room, we could watch her as she goes in. I've got a security pass. What do you think? That might be nice, just to see what she looks like with her hair done and everything. And you'll have a chance to look round the director's box.'

The auditions manager said it was OK and, a little while later, Dad led them out of the hall and along various corridors until they came to a door marked DIRECTOR.

'Here we are,' he said.

He swiped his card and they went in.

It was a small technical-looking room filled with computers, screens and control panels. Down one side of it there was a long window looking out onto a large, square room hung with spotlights and set up with cameras.

'A Sony HDW-750P!' Laura said.

'The control centre!' Marcus said.

'Buttons!' said Tug.

Dad explained that the window was a mirror on the other side, so that what happened in the director's box didn't disturb the actors out in the studio. It was sound-proofed too. He pointed through the window. 'The audition room's on the far side of the studio, through that door over there. We'll be able to see Martha as she goes across. Tug,' he added, 'don't push the buttons.'

'This is where it happens,' Marcus murmured to Laura. 'This is where the power resides. I can feel it.'

They were so busy looking at everything that they

didn't realize what time it was until they heard footsteps in the corridor outside. Dad looked at his watch.

'Quarter past already,' he said. 'She must be about to go in. Quick!'

They crowded to the window to get the best view of her.

But no one came into the studio. Instead, the door behind them was suddenly flung open, and Grandma and Grandpa burst into the director's box, followed by Alison from the Social Services and the auditions manager.

'Just as I told you!' Grandma cried. And there was a commotion.

Tug had seen Grandma angry before so he wasn't surprised. But Marcus was.

'Dear lady,' he said, putting a hand on her arm. 'She hasn't gone in yet. You're just in time to see her.'

'Don't touch me, you degenerate,' she said. 'I'm here to stop her.'

Tug watched them all arguing. Alison from Social Services was telling Dad something about the penalties for court order violation, and Dad was asking Grandma to please, please just listen to him, and Grandpa was looking for his glasses which he had dropped, and Marcus was muttering 'Degenerate? Degenerate?' in a half-shocked, half-pleased sort of way; and in general everyone was speaking and no one was listening, and the noise grew louder and louder until in the end Tug had to get up on the desk and shout to make himself heard.

'Quiet!' he shouted, and everyone stopped to look at him.

'There she is!' he said, pointing.

At exactly the same moment they all turned to look out of the window, and no one spoke as they watched Martha in the studio beyond.

She was on her own, and she walked with slow, quiet steps, head up, from one side of the studio to the other. She was wearing Marcus's brilliantly ugly dress, and the braids of her hair shone, and as she pointed her small nose from side to side, looking about her, she seemed brave and hopeful and very nervous all at once. At the door to the audition room she paused and seemed to give a little sigh of determination. Then she knocked and went in, and shut the door behind her.

There was silence in the director's box.

'My little girl,' Grandma said in a broken voice.

They all turned to look at her. She was holding on

316

to Grandpa, and her face was white. 'Just the same,' she whispered.

'I know,' Grandpa said.

'The same look on her face.'

'Hush,' he said. 'Don't cry.'

Dad took Grandma's hand. 'She would have been so proud of her,' he said. 'Won't you let her audition?'

And Grandma nodded.

47

Later that afternoon all the families were waiting in the performers' room for the candidates to return from the audition office, where they had been called to hear the director's verdicts.

One by one they came back in, each holding an envelope. The murmur of voices steadily grew. There were some tears. People began to leave.

Still Martha didn't appear.

Everyone was tense.

'Dad?' Tug whispered.

'What?'

'I'm still wondering where the canteen is.'

'Not now, Tug.'

'I'm wondering very hard.'

'In a minute.'

Finally she came.

They all fell silent as she joined them. She stood there for a moment looking at their expectant faces – Dad and Tug, Marcus and Laura,

318

Grandma and Grandpa – and smiled.

It was a brave smile.

'I didn't get it,' she said. 'Sorry.'

They all began to talk at once, and Martha could hear herself saying, 'It's OK, I don't mind.'

But the truth was, she did. It surprised her, how much she minded. She hadn't even expected to get the part.

Everyone crowded round her talking, but she wasn't listening. She was lost in her own thoughts. It felt to her as if she'd failed again. Suddenly she didn't think that Mum would have been proud of her. She thought that she'd let down Marcus and Laura, and she was worried that Grandma was going to be very cross, and she was frightened that Dad was going to get into trouble for helping her. Worst of all, she felt sorry for herself, she couldn't help it.

Ordinarily, she was good at controlling herself. But somehow she couldn't do it any more. After all the times in the last two years she'd managed to keep her head, it seemed such a small, selfish thing to make her upset now. It was as if all the emotions she'd pushed down inside her for so long were rising up, and she couldn't stop them. Tears sprang into her eyes, and she started to gulp. There was no possibility now of keeping her head. No possibility of closing her eyes and taking a deep breath, of making a list and carrying on as normal. Her chin began to tremble and her hands began to shake, and she turned to Dad to be comforted.

But Dad wasn't there.

She looked round, confused. He'd promised he'd be there whenever she needed him.

'Tug?' she said.

At first Tug wasn't there either. Then she saw him sidle in through the door at the far side of the room, and she left the others and ran over to him.

'Where have you been, Tug? Where's Dad?'

'He went, Martha.'

'Where did he go?'

'Not to the canteen,' Tug said sadly.

She was confused.

'I thought he was going to the canteen,' Tug said. 'That's why I followed him. But he went to that other place.'

'What other place?'

Tug tried to remember its name. 'The bar,' he said at last.

Martha flinched. 'The *bar*?'

'He said he couldn't wait, Martha.'

Now she wasn't crying any more. She stood there, breathing heavily. Her eyes were bright and fierce, and her heart was pounding.

'What did he look like, Tug, when he said he was going to the bar?'

'A bit . . . strange.'

'What about his face? Was it pale and shiny?'

Tug nodded.

'And his hands? Did he run them through his hair?'

He nodded again. He peered at Martha timidly. 'Are you all right, Martha? Your face is very red.'

Her face felt red. And her lungs felt as if they were about to burst. 'I trusted him!' she said. 'I'll *never* trust him again!' She glared at Tug so fiercely he shrank away from her. 'Do you remember the way to the bar?'

He nodded fearfully.

'Take me. Quickly!'

The staff bar – Cheers! – was on the second floor, next to the New Moon Café canteen. In a corner booth, Dad was sitting talking to the director of *Anne of Green Gables*. Luckily he had known where to find him. They had met once before, a few years earlier, and when Dad came running up and introduced himself again, the director remembered him and said he was happy to talk about the auditioning.

He was a big, sensible man with a suntan, and he was drinking a glass of Californian Pinot Noir, which he said reminded him of home, while Dad sipped a cup of tea.

'You want to know why we didn't offer her the part?'

'I'd just like to give her some feedback. She's my daughter, I know, but I think she's got something special, and she's so thoughtful and bright she'd listen to any advice you might have. I can't stay long.' He looked anxiously at his watch. 'I have to get back to her.'

'Well, I'll tell you straight,' the director said. 'When I first saw her I thought we had it all sewn up. Wow, the kid can act. You know that. Looks just right too. She did a piece from early on in the book, where Anne imagines all the fancy stuff in the room. Stunning. Best performance I've seen. Knockout, really. But the second piece didn't work out so well.'

'Which piece was that?'

'One of the tantrum scenes. A real stamper and shouter. I don't know why it didn't work, but it didn't. Technically, she was superb. But I couldn't feel the emotion. It wasn't coming through. And, you know, those scenes are real important to the book. That fierceness of spirit – it's who Anne is. I'm looking for someone who can really let rip when she needs to.'

It was at that moment that Martha appeared. Still wearing her ugly dress of yellowish-grey wincey, her face tear-streaked and furious, she came up to the side of the booth at speed and, without pausing to look round, addressed Dad in a loud voice.

'You couldn't wait? You couldn't wait to start drinking again?'

Startled, Dad made an attempt to introduce the director, but Martha cut him off.

'I believed you when you told me you'd stopped. I won't ever believe you again. Not ever! What would Mum think of you? What will Tug think of you when he's bigger? As soon as things go wrong, you give up. What are you going to do – kill yourself, like Laura's dad?'

Very embarrassed, Dad attempted again to explain.

'I hate you!' she shouted. 'I hate you! You lied to me. And you lied to yourself. You're a coward and a cheat.'

'Martha,' Dad began, very red in the face.

'Do you think *I* don't want to give up sometimes?'

she shouted at him. 'I tried to look after Tug, and I tried to help you, and I worked as hard as I could to audition for that part so that Mum could have been pleased with *something* I did. And nothing went right, ever. I feel so bad I could cry. But I'm not going to. Because now I know something. It's better to try and fail than give up, like you do, running away and coming in here just so you could drink *that*!'

And she pointed dramatically at the glass in his hand.

And realized at once that it wasn't a glass, but a teacup.

And anyway ran out of breath, and stood there with fierce, confused eyes, gasping.

And the director, whom she hadn't even noticed until then, stood up – he was a very big man, very suntanned, and it gave her a real shock to see him there – and put out his big hand. Without thinking she shook it as politely as she could, still panting, with her face all wet and red.

'Congratulations, Miss Luna,' he said. 'You've got the part.'

48

It was 2.30 p.m., and they were all sitting together in the New Moon Café: Martha, Tug, Dad, Marcus, Laura, Grandma, Grandpa, Alison and the big Californian director.

The New Moon Café was the television studio's staff canteen. It was friendly and smart, with white tables and red chairs, and lights with pretty green shades. In the serving area at the far end there were glass-fronted display cabinets full of hot and cold food, and fridges with desserts and drinks in them, and on the walls above were menus advertising specials: pasta dishes, salads and different sorts of pie.

Looking round, Martha noticed the moon theme. There were jaunty little moons on the napkins, and bouncing moons round the lampshades, and moons on the doors, and the menus, and the backs of the seats. Round the walls were large framed cartoons of moons. There was a man in the moon drinking a milkshake from a straw, and a dish and spoon

325

jumping over the moon. And, in the corner, there was a big slice of moon pie served up on a plate.

She turned to point it out to Tug, but he was busy talking to the cook, who was describing the day's specials to them.

'I like mince and onion,' he was saying, 'but my *favourite* is steak and kidney.'

'Well, would you believe it?' the cook said. 'Steak and kidney is today's special.' She was a large lady with bright eyes. 'And we've more than a dozen portions left.'

'What's dozen?' Tug asked.

'Twelve.'

He turned in his seat and bellowed happily across the table, 'At last, Martha! Someone who understands me.'

Everyone was busy talking, Martha noticed. It was like a birthday party.

Marcus was talking to the director about costumes. 'Do you agree,' he was saying, 'that sometimes it really has to knock your eye out, and sometimes it just hasn't?'

And the director was saying, 'You're a very astute young man. What was the name of your company again?'

Grandma was talking to Dad about Mum. 'I have all her old outfits in the attic,' she was saying. 'Stored very neatly. I wonder if Martha would like to have them.'

And Laura was telling Grandpa and Alison how the Sony HDW-750P worked.

Martha sat back in her seat, and let all the talk wash over her. She had the strangest feeling, a sort of melty feeling in her tummy, and a ticklish feeling around her mouth. After a while she realized what it was. She was happy.

She caught Dad's eye, and they looked at each other. Grandma was still talking to him, but he'd stopped listening. For a moment he looked as if he was going to say something to Martha, and then he looked as if he wasn't. And for a moment she looked as if she was about to take a deep breath, the way she used to, and then she didn't.

They both smiled instead.

Acknowledgements

Heartfelt thanks to my editor, Bella Pearson, who made this book better. And love to Eluned, Gwilym and Eleri, who make everything else better.